WEALTH *of the* WICKED

AN AMERICAN TRAGEDY OF ELDERLY ABUSE

JANICE M. LAUDERDALE

IBSN-10: 0-9774852-2-6

Published by: Urban Classic Books
6245 Bristol Parkway #265
Culver City, CA 90230
www.urbanclassicbooks.com
Contact author: www.writethewrong1.com

Printed in USA
Email: janicelauderdale@yahoo.com
Library of Congress Catalog Card No: In publication data

FOREWORD

By La Joy Henry

THROUGH THE EYES OF THE OFFENDED

The authenticity of this book was born out of passion and a desire for vindication and justice. It gives voice to the betrayed and offended. It tells the sorrowful story of betrayal to the innocent and brings justification to that life. If the law doesn't fully bring justice, then the writer expresses it here from her own sense of vindication. The writer speaks from the heart to release her feelings and thoughts in order to survive and move on with life.

By the writer expressing the depth of her anguish, anger and disgust, the reader experiences the crime first hand. It gives insight into the world of betrayal and darkness inhabited by deceptive predators that prey on the helpless and vulnerable. They hunt for prey like wild animals that attack only the sick, weak and helpless. They, like thieves, prey on the elderly under the guise of love and on the premise that they are the only ones looking out for their welfare. They have an immoral sense of gratification in thinking that they have gotten over on someone, but in fact, our moral society frowns upon such behavior. "THE THIEF COMES NOT BUT FOR TO KILL, STEAL, AND DESTROY...."

This book gives voice to millions who have encountered predatory injustice, and for those unable to speak for themselves. Its pathos enlightens and reveals the subtlety of the deceptive predator, which serves to warn the public to become aware of the intent of those who say, "I love you."

Testimonials

In a world in which knowledge truly is the commodity of kings, *"Wealth of the Wicked: An American Tragedy of Elderly Abuse,"* is a real life case study exposing in vivid detail the injustices perpetrated against individuals experiencing diminishing capacities in their twilight years. The engaging volume is replete with substantive information and facts, including ten safeguards for protecting the elderly. A must read!
— Dr. Darnell Holmes, Pastor First United Methodist Church
Compton, California

* * *

Wealth Of The Wicked: An American Tragedy of Elderly Abuse is dynamic, and the writing prolific. It is clearly written and eye-opening. The ten signs of elder abuse are great for training, educating and informing the public. I am enthralled, but also shocked at how your Lucille character, who should be held in high esteem, so easily becomes a victim of her own family member. Thank God for your courage to face and challenge this tragedy, and overcome it. You give a supreme lesson in courage and bravery. The book should become required reading for loved ones, caregivers, and nonprofit agencies that deal with the elderly.
— Dr. Kerry S. Brooks, Professor Counseling and Psychology

* * *

Courageous, intense, liberating, and victorious. "Wealth of the Wicked: An American Tragedy of Elderly Abuse," gives insight to the tentacles of deceit and the chaos of greed. The author iluminates the pain of betrayal and offers resolve for the hearts of those determined to hold fast to the true meaning of family.
— Dr. Nicole LaBeach, Author of *"A Woman's True Purpose: Live Like You Matter"* and CEO of Volition Enterprises, Inc.
www.drlabeach.com

Dedication

Every good work involves sacrifice, and this book is no exception. I offer my sincere appreciation to my book Coach and nurturer, Martha Tucker of the award-winning novel, *The Mayor's Wife Wore Sapphires*. You took me by the hand, put me on track and kept me there until Wealth of the Wicked was finished.

To my family—my husband Dennis, and my children Candace and Ryan, without you this book would not have been written. Each, in your own way, has been pillars of strength. You proved what strong family ties feel like. At times, my way became very bleak, a personal horror, but you never abandoned me. Even when I was so anguished that I repeated myself over and over again, you allowed let me get it out. That was therapy for me, and I thank you.

To my sister LaJoy Henry, you were indeed the closest blood tie to me in this fiasco. You never lost sight of the fact that a grave injustice had been done to an innocent person. You knew and understood. Although many miles separated us, I thank you for standing with me and for your undying loyalty during that time.

To my dear cousin Agnes Crawford, my heart still bleeds for what you endured through the events on which this story is based. I am grateful that you knew I did my best for you and your granddaughter Dajah. Your tenacity and loyalty never waivered. Agnes, may the peace of God continue to rest upon your life as He continues to guide you to the safe places. You are the best, loved by so many, myself included.

Opening Statement

"It was someone I trusted—a blood relative. This book is about the loss of that relationship. What I learned during that horror was the lengths to which some people will go to take what does not belong to them. They have no moral compass. They abandon every right principle to accomplish their selfish goals: To have the wealth that belongs to others. The art of greed.   In this case, it was the art of greed against the most innocent—the elderly."

Chapter 1

Summer 2005: Dear God, I write in my diary because I need to make sense of what is happening in my life. You know I'm a mature woman now, and I find myself in a situation that I don't understand. I toss and turn, and scream at night, as I see this thing over and over again. I need your help. Help me.
Your loving daughter, Danielle.

In the warmth of that summer afternoon, I could feel the end of summer in the air, and couldn't wait to return to Greenleaf Junior High. I longed to be back with my friends. It was 1962, I was fourteen, and going into the 9th grade.

As I daydreamed about showing off new penny loafers and bobby sox at school, I also thought of wrapping my tongue around the black walnut ice cream in the refrigerator. I opened the freezer door, and the cold frosty air hit my face. Even before my tongue could touch it, the rich, nutty flavor mesmerized me. I ripped the hard block of deliciousness from the box marked, Dream Day Dairy–Black Walnut. The rich smell of walnuts heightened my desire to taste it. I dug out two scoops and began to eat. Ah, the velvety, smooth coldness! The taste of crunchy walnuts and textured flavors was everything I had expected. I put another scoop into my bowl.

I walked back into the dining room and took a seat on the floor, pulling an unfinished jumbo crossword puzzle from the bureau drawer. As I lay on my stomach and began to fill in the blank squares, the door banged open. My brother Drake stood there, breathing fire. He was only two years older than me, but his six-foot two frame always made me feel smaller than my five feet four inch skinny self. Drake's dark skin, deceptive brown eyes and growling voice always gave me the feeling I'd been grabbed by a pit bull's locking jaws. I felt pinned in.

"Where'd you get that?" Drake pointed to my ice cream.

"From the fridge," I said, taking another big bite, for fear that he might snatch it at any second.

"Who told you you could eat that? Huh? Who told you?"

"It was in the freezer," I sassed, while stuffing my mouth.

He got right in my ear and yelled, "It wasn't yours; it was mine!"

My hearing went deaf for a minute, and my 14-year-old body shook, not so much from fear as from disdain. His yelling ran hot through my entire body, and my thoughts ran back to the fights he always started. If today was going to be anything like the past, this Wilt Chamberlain look-alike would pin me against the wall and punch me until I nearly fainted.

"I'mma tell momma."

I stuffed my mouth with another big spoonful, but it no longer tasted special. It went down tasting like sawdust. As Drake's size 10 tennis shoes tore into the kitchen, where momma was fixing dinner, the walls vibrated.

"Why's Danielle eating my ice cream?" He yelled. Something slammed that sounded like a pan hitting the wall, or his fist slamming something. All of my insides quivered, not knowing what he might do. I had a flash of him hitting my mother. I ran into the kitchen to see what was going on. Momma was fixing dinner, ignoring him, and Drake stomped toward the refrigerator like a speeding freight train on the wrong track. He snatched the freezer door open, grabbed the ice cream, and threw the quart container outside. It sailed through the air like in slow motion. The delicious, creamy coldness hit the ground with a thud. I was glad my younger sisters were in the back room and didn't see that. It was too ugly, too angry, and too awful.

I couldn't understand why anyone would rather throw away ice cream from the Dream Day Dairy than to allow his own sister to eat it. My brain looped into more particles from the past. Over the darkness of Drake's beatings and arrogance, the black storms of his wrath almost took my breath away. Our three-bedroom house, with one bathroom, must have heard this kind of ruckus many times before. The larger bedroom with two sets of bunk beds and two chests of drawers was where my three sisters and I slept. Drake, the only boy, had his own bedroom.

Then he slammed the kitchen door and stalked into his room. The noise was so loud that our modest lower middle-class neighborhood must have heard it. The bashing sound took me back to his past meanness. In the one bathroom that all of us shared, no one could linger, except Drake. Often, when I would knock on the bathroom door, Drake would laugh or whistle nonchalantly as I hopped from one foot to the other, yelling, "I got to use it!"

Dancing a jig back to my bedroom, dribbling urine in a dotted line, I was too embarrassed to wet my clothes entirely. I called for help.

"Momma, Momma, I got to use it!"

When momma started down the hall, Drake would open the door, smiling deceitfully.

"Did you need to come in, sis?"

Now, when he turned from tossing the ice cream, he had the same deceitful smile on his face. My brain settled a bit and focused on our family philosophy—anything in the refrigerator, except for momma's Pepsi, belonged to everyone in the house. My father made sure we had plenty of food, and no one went hungry. It was never "my food" versus "your food." Food in our house belonged to all of us, and Drake was supposed to know that.

When Drake reached his room, he stuck his tongue out at me. That seething anger and uncontrollable rage leapt off him like a blaze. I just stood there, shocked into silence. I decided then that there was no end to what Drake would do to hurt me.

Chapter 2

August 13, 1984: Dear God, Drake is home after spending 20 years in the United States Marine Corps. He says he is honorably discharged, but I'm not sure about that. Anyhow, he has returned to California—to my parent's home. I didn't want him to come and disturb their lives, but...he's here, Lord.... I wrote for an hour before I stopped.

I looked at Drake across the room in the house where we grew up, wondering whether he had changed. Could he be a real brother? I noticed that he had the same arrogant stride when he walked, and that surly reply to every question. He wore a deceitful broad smile and a lifetime of lies lodged in those high cheeks. They seemed to be made for storing lies.

When he walked past me, I said, "I hope you've changed."

"I don't need to change. Worry about yourself. Who are you anyway?"

That was my answer. He was as arrogant as ever, and I was as disgusted with him as ever. Drake had always been a person who wanted the easy way out. My motto: No pain, no gain. His motto: Your pain, my gain.

"I heard you made some kind of mess in the Marines and got out as quick as you could," I said.

Seeing him pass me, after 20 years, and knowing the man he was before going into the service, I knew the rumors were true. He didn't achieve a higher rank than sergeant in all those years. First of all, he could never listen to anyone, and the Marine Corps was about rules, regulations, and then rank. I had a good visual of him imprinted on my mind: his commanding officers issuing orders to a man who had spent a lifetime trying to alter rules, make new rules, or downright disobey the rules. I imagined Drake shuffling off, rolling his eyes, mumbling back, or going out the door and doing the opposite. He was always looking for ways to go around the rules.

Drake would give the impression that he was interested in my mother's or father's words of wisdom, but his listening was just the means to an end. It was always about Drake getting what he wanted. He would go right out the door and do the opposite of what they suggested. I had tired of dealing with him long ago.

Life in the inner city had changed while Drake was away in the service. Nineteen-sixty five had ushered in the worst riot Los Angeles had ever known. During that era, two great leaders were brutally assassinated—Dr. Martin Luther King, Jr., and Attorney General Robert Kennedy. Now, after twenty years in the service, Drake couldn't support himself. With duffle bag on his shoulder, he had moved back home. He said it was only for a short stay, but the short stay ended up being two years. During that time, he married for the second time, and finally moved out. I was so relieved when he moved out!

I shouldn't have gotten relieved quite so fast. Six years later, he divorced wife number two and, once again, he had to find a place to live. Of course, he returned to our parents' home. He just couldn't seem to make it on his own. Unfortunately, my parents tolerated him and his arrogance, my father much more than my mother. He even had the gall to buy food and put it in the room where he slept, with no regard for my mother's rules about no food in the bedrooms. He was stuck in his own principles of, "My room. My stuff!"

When my dad complained to me about Drake, I would say to him, "Dad, this isn't the conversation you should be having with me. You need to talk to your son, personally."

My dad was a passive man, and that just wasn't something he wanted to do. I'm almost thinking my dad never thought his son, my brother, would turn out like he did. He so much wanted to see the best in him. But he'd have to look very, very hard! The best wasn't easily found.

* * *

September 20, 2000:   Dear God, my heart is beginning to feel a part of a new life around me. Something strange is happening. I hope it's the good I need to hear....

My 79-year-old dad had suffered a heart attack, and was later diagnosed with congestive heart failure. When he experienced chest pains, my brother took him to Buena Vista Hospital. Later, his other children came to visit him. My dad enjoyed all of the attention. He loved his family! After being in the hospital for approximately four days, he was released to come home with instructions and medication.

Now, my dad had been retired for twenty years and was living on a fixed income. He and his wife of 56 years, my mother,

Lorena, lived on that income. They managed their limited resources—that is, until their son Drake returned home. That put a heavy strain on their budget. It became more and more difficult to get Drake to pay them the meager $200 he had promised them each month, and to get it paid on time. Then my mother lost her lifetime partner, and she went into mourning. My mother's relationship with Drake had reached an all-time low.

Five years earlier, mom and dad had decided to take out a reverse mortgage on their house. This allowed them to live a little more comfortably, and they got a little stipend each month, in addition to being able to get needed repairs done to their home. My father had said that he wanted our youngest sister Brenda, if she was able, to pay the house out of the reverse mortgage and have a place for her and her son to live.

Before Brenda made an attempt at the reverse mortgage, Drake, for some reason, was given two opportunities to pay the house out of the reverse mortgage. Maybe it had something to do with him being the first-born. He tried twice, and he failed twice. Poor credit! Even then, he did the less than honorable thing. He told our mother that she had to pay a realtor $3,000 to complete the transaction. He never paid back the money he borrowed from her. When the last attempt to get the loan paid out of the reverse mortgage failed, mom asked him for the money.

"You don't need no money," he barked.

Now, just how do you tell your mother she doesn't need her money? I wanted only one thing—for Drake to leave my mom's house. I looked for a way for that to happen. I was overjoyed when I heard that Brenda would attempt to buy the house out of the reverse mortgage. She deserved it. Brenda had demonstrated her love for mom and dad over the years.

Brenda shared with me that Drake, after failing to qualify for the reverse mortgage, suggested that *"they"* purchase the house together. Before he could get it out of his mouth, Brenda said, "You must be crazy."

* * *

April 12, 2004: Dear God, life seems so tangled right now. Please give me clarity.

Brenda retrieved the house from the reverse mortgage. Now she was a homeowner, and had the American dream! During the time she was preparing to move into her new house, Drake was still living with mom, and rest assured, he wasn't going to live there when Brenda and her son moved in. Now, time was Drake's immediate enemy.

Chapter 3

June 16, 2004: Dear God, I am still shocked over the turn of events in my life, when all I wanted was peace and a loving family, now here I am again....

My father's oldest sister, Lucille, age 87, lived alone in her green and white house on the south side of 85th and Menlo. She had lived there for 52 years, and after her husband died, she had never moved. Whenever I asked Lucille, "Why don't you let me get someone to come in and help you?" she always gave the same answer.

"Cause I don't want nobody in my house doing nothin' for me." Her voice was brash and untamed. And as if I hadn't heard her the first time, she'd repeat, "I don't want nobody to come in and do nothin' for me."

"Lucille, I think it's time for someone to give you a little help."

Lucille would hear nothing of it. And, because I knew it was the right time to get help for her, I asked again at other times. "What about somebody living with you just to make sure you're safe at night?"

"Heavens, no! I don't want nobody in my house doing nothing for me."

Back in the day when Lucille was beautiful and able-bodied, she would give anybody a go for their money. Age aside, she wasn't backing down, and she was becoming annoyed with me.

"Danielle, I told you I can still clean. I still cook my own food."

I wasn't buying it because I knew better. So I made a proposal. "OK. You find a friend to come and live with you."

"I been living by myself all these years. I can't live with nobody."

"Yes, I know you want to keep on doing things the way you've always done them, but I think it would be safer." I pleaded with her, "Won't you just consider it?"

Lucille's mind was set. I couldn't get her to change. "Don't bring nobody in my house."

"Well, I—"

"I'll do it till I can't."

"Okay, have it your way." Now, thinking back, I should have taken control and had my way. I was the one who was mentally acute at the time. But ever since childhood I always wanted to please her.

In July 2002, Drake started visiting Lucille regularly. He soon started taking Lucille to the grocery store, which my father had done until he died. Lucille enjoyed having Drake take her brother's place and take her to the stores, as she suffered from arthritis in both knees. As time wore on and age began taking over, Lucille consented to making a list of things she wanted from the market. Drake was right there to fulfill her needs and wishes. He'd rub her knees with healing creams and stroke her legs.

"You know, Auntie, why don't you think about me being here with you all the time. That way I can help you whenever you need me."

"Umm," she said.

"I can cook for you. Go to the store for you. Auntie, I'll take real good care of you."

Was Lucille really listening to Drake? From the way she was talking to me, she'd been swept away by the smooth talk and soothing cream Drake applied to her knees. Did he mistake her head nod for a "yes?"

It was obvious that Lucille was going to need assistance with her daily living—bathing, dressing, shopping, and preparing meals, for sure. There were offers of someone moving in to care for her, and there was also an offer from Meals-On-Wheels. She wouldn't hear of it! "If you get those Meals-On-Wheels, I ain't gonna eat that s—t."

So, checking in on her almost daily was the next best thing. Her niece Isabelle vowed to call Lucille every night. Isabelle couldn't drive and take Lucille places, but she kept her promise to call and check on her aunt daily. On most occasions, when Isabelle was unable to call, one of her grandchildren would call Lucille to make sure she was okay.

Then, on June 16, 2004, I got a call from Isabelle. She hadn't been able to reach Lucille for more than two days, and she was worried. She wanted to know if I had spoken with her. I told her that I hadn't.

There was no need to panic because often Lucille wouldn't answer her phone if she didn't feel like it. After one occasion, I said to her, "I tried to call you yesterday, but the phone just rang and rang."

"Oh, yeah, I was here," she said.

There was no need to pursue that conversation any further. It would do no good.

But this time, Isabelle's voice told me something wasn't quite right. "Danielle, I'm worried."

I called one of Lucille's long-time neighbors, and asked her if she would go across the street and knock on Lucille's door. In a half-hour, the neighbor called me back and said there was no answer. Anxiety sprang up in me, so I decided to go over to Lucille's house myself. My husband Spencer drove and my son Travis joined us. They tried to unlock the front door with my key, but the door wouldn't open. The neighbors gathered, milling around, mumbling about how much they loved Lucille.

Then, while Travis and I tried to unlock the front door, my husband decided to go to the bathroom window on the west side of the house. He began chanting, "Aunt Lucille, Aunt Lucille, can you hear me? Can you hear me?" He got a little bit closer to the window and thought he heard a faint voice coming from the bathroom. It was Lucille. She was in some kind of trouble, for sure. She was grunting faintly. Travis and I hurried over to the bathroom window.

"Lucille, we're here," I said.

The bathroom window had a little crack in it, and we kept hearing the faint noise, something like heavy breathing. The opening in the bathroom window was too small to enter. Instead, my son took the keys and attempted to open the sliding glass door in the rear den. It worked. Travis rushed into the bathroom, and I followed. We found Lucille lying in the bathtub. She reeked of urine and feces, and looked weak and pale. It looked like she had been in the bathtub for days. I remembered when she had refused to allow me to put safety bars in the tub.

Lucille's next-door neighbor began yelling at my son, "Get outta her house. Get out. I'm calling the police!" Someone said his name was Elroy. He was a small, dark man with a pot gut and a brash voice.

"That's my son," I called to him.

"I'm calling the police to have you arrested for burglary."

"That's our son," I called louder.

My concern was getting Lucille out of the bathtub's contaminated water.

"We're getting you out, Lucille. You're going to be fine."

Spencer and Travis pulled Lucille from the feces and urine polluted water. She was cold and disoriented. I called 911.

When the paramedics arrived, Lucille looked water-logged. Her skin was shriveled and as white as a sheet. She was shivering, speaking in a whisper. I removed her wet clothes and washed her body, then moved her into her bedroom to dress her in dry clothes. She complained of severe pain in her right hand.

"How long were you in the tub?" one of the paramedics asked.

She said nothing while Elroy, the obnoxious neighbor, moved in, trying to talk to Lucille while the paramedics talked to her.

"Lucille, this is Elroy. I love you." He pushed toward the bed.

I didn't understand why he had to be there. He was in no way related to her. And what was the *"I love you"* about? With four paramedics and myself in the small room, there was just no room for him.

"Sir, you have to leave, so we can do our job," one of the paramedics said.

The neighbor stalked out, grumbling. He stopped and picked up Lucille's phone and called the police to report a burglary, accusing my son of being the suspect.

The paramedics continued working on Lucille. "Lucille, you were in a bathtub."

"Yeah," she said weakly.

"How long were you in the bathtub?"

"I don't know."

"How did you get into the tub?"

Lucille was trying to come up with a different answer, but to no avail. The fear on her face was frightening. I got really worried. Things didn't look good. The paramedics picked her up and rushed out. We agreed to take her to Mayfair Medical in South Gate. My husband and I followed the ambulance. I wondered if that was the last time I would ever see Lucille alive.

Chapter 4

June 20, 2004: Dear God, the pain of all this is making me ill. I can't sleep or eat. It's affecting my entire family. I need to see a way through this.... Danielle wrote in the diary until it was dark, got up from the doorstep, and walked inside.

At 2 o'clock that next afternoon, I drove in the humid summer sunshine to Mayfair to see Lucille, as I had done for the past three days. This time of year, when thoughts turn to summer vacations, the usual picnics and fireworks brought no joy. I walked into Lucille's room after pasting a smile on my face. I didn't like seeing her look so frail. She straightened the blue housecoat over her chest, leaned back, and turned her face toward the window. I didn't know if she recognized me.

"Hi, Aunt Lucille."

She knew someone was in the room with her. Whether she knew it was me or not, was another story. Then she turned her head towards the door and saw me. I gave her the biggest smile, and she smiled back faintly. What a relief!

"How are you?"

"My hand hurts." She grasped it and held it out for me to see.

"I'm sorry. Are they giving you something for the pain?"

"I don't know."

"I'll check with the nurse."

"Okay."

"Other than your hand hurting, are you alright?"

"Yeah. I just wanna go home."

"I know you do, but you have to wait until the doctor says it's okay."

"Danielle, I don't know what I would do without you."

"I'm here for you."

Finally, the nurse peeked into Lucille's room and said she was going to be transferred. Lucille managed a smile, assuming the nurse's words were good news.

"To where?" I asked.

"To Genesis Acute Rehabilitation Center. It's a nice place," the nurse smiled.

The next day, in the early afternoon, Lucille was transferred. The doctor gave me an appointment to meet with the charge nurse the following day to discuss Lucille's after-discharge plans. Lucille made sure I knew she didn't want to stay there. She wanted to go home.

"Lucille, you can't go home until the doctor releases you, okay?"

"Well, when they gonna release me?"

"I don't know."

"Who's gonna release me?"

"The doctor."

"When?"

"He'll let you know. They promise not to keep you here any longer than they have to, okay?"

"Okay."

"Do you understand what I'm telling you?"

"Yeah."

For the moment, she seemed soothed, knowing she would be going home soon.

* * *

On June 22, I arrived early at Genesis for a 1:30 p.m. appointment. Lucille and I were supposed to meet with the discharge nurse to discuss plans for her after-discharge medical care.

When I went to Lucille's room, she was not at all up to attending a meeting.

"Danielle, do I have to go?"

"Yes, Aunt Lucille. This meeting is for you."

"For what?"

"The nurse is going to talk about what I need to do for you after you leave here."

"But, do I have to go?"

"Yes."

She reluctantly agreed and told me she was cold. I put her favorite beige sweater on her, which I had brought with me. It had seen better days, but today it would do just fine.

After the meeting, the nurse rolled Lucille back to her room. She looked depressed. She didn't want to do anything besides stay in bed. The nurses begged her to eat with the other patients and participate in activities, but she wouldn't hear of it. I was unable to convince her that it would be good for her—she wasn't buying it. I picked up my purse and the bag I had used to bring her sweater.

"Lucille, I'm leaving."

"Okay. When you coming back?"

"I'll be back tomorrow."

"Okay, Danielle."

Chapter 5

Danielle sat up in her bed and wrote her note to God.

June 23, 2004: Dear God, as promised, I made my way back to Genesis today. I just don't know how all of this will turn out. I've always loved my father's sister, but I'm feeling uneasy about her future. Very uneasy. Danielle kept writing….

The next morning was a typical sunny Southern California day. With the sun beaming down on me and knowing Lucille was in a good place, I felt invigorated. I made my way to Lucille's room. After we exchanged pleasantries, the doctor came in. I wasn't prepared for what he said. He stood between Lucille and me, crossed his arms, and looked me straight in the eyes. Doctors always do that when they're about to lower the boom.

"Mrs. Carrington," he said, rocking back and forth on his heels and toes. "She can't live alone any longer."

My brain froze for a moment, then lurched forward a thousand miles a minute. Who in the world could I find to move in with her? My husband and I were building a business. It was our jobs, our livelihood. If we didn't work, we didn't eat. My children were in school. The doctor's earth-shattering news left me speechless. My mind was racing faster than a race car at the Indy 500. I was trying to be careful not to let Lucille know my thoughts while I silently pondered the dilemma.

"Oh, God, what shall I do?" I mumbled to myself.

The doctor left, leaving behind a huge pile of mental debris. There was no one I could think of to go to and ask, "Do you think you can make room for Lucille to move in with you?" There was absolutely no one! Not my sisters. Not my mother. Not my cousins. So I kept pondering my predicament.

I was reeling from the doctor's news. But evidently Lucille had already been told she couldn't live alone anymore, because after I had been knocked off my feet with the news, Lucille leaned over and whispered to me.

"Drake's going to move in with me. Ain't that good?"

Drake! Oh, my God. That was a solution, but I knew it was a solution straight out of hell. But then, this was his aunt. His father's oldest sister. I sat on the edge of her bed, looked her squarely in the face, and said, "Are you sure, Aunt Lucille? You sure you want Drake to come and live with you?"

"Yeaaaaaaah."

Well, it was the 11th hour, and if not him, who?

On June 24, the day before Lucille was to be discharged, Drake and I happened to visit Lucille at the same time. When I arrived, he was already there. As a matter of fact, soon after I arrived, he left. I didn't know how long he had been there, and certainly didn't know what they had talked about. Neither Lucille nor I had a clue as to how this arrangement would work out. I left the hospital with the weight of Lucille's world on my shoulders.

Chapter 6

Danielle walked into the kitchen when the house was quiet and talked into her tape recorder.

June 25, 2004: Dear God, you know Drake, and so do I. I'm worried. Help me to be of assistance to Lucille in this situation....

Drake picked up Lucille from Genesis Acute Rehabilitation Center on that nice warm day full of hazy sunshine and brought her home. I was in Lucille's bedroom changing her bed when they arrived. I brought a broad smile to the front door to greet Lucille, but she wasn't smiling. She looked like a mixture of emotions—tired and glad at the same time. Even the drive from the hospital probably made her tired. The gladness must have come from being back in the security of her home. Why shouldn't she feel safe? She had earned it.

She had made the arrangements with Drake, and there was no changing Lucille's mind once she had made it up. Drake would move in with her as *caretaker.* Is she going to be okay? I kept wondering. Each step she made was like a person moving in slow motion. That told me Drake wasn't the one to take care of her. But she managed to get to her *old faithful,* her favorite green folding chair.

Although Lucille had discussed the pay arrangement with Drake, she seemed uncomfortable with the arrangement when

Drake asked her about it. "We agreed on the six hundred bucks a month, so I'd like to get an advance."

"I don't remember that," Lucille said, as Drake walked into the back of the house.

"Is that right, Lucille?" I asked.

"He shouldn't get nothing–I'll be paying for everything. He'll be staying here and not paying no rent." Lucille didn't seem to like that idea one bit!

Drake returned. "Actually, you told me six fifty!"

"I didn't tell you no such thing."

I thought to myself, if Drake hadn't been talking to Lucille about this, who had he talked to? I had handled all of her business for years, and he had sneaked behind my back and made some kind of deal with Lucille, and she had moved ahead without me witnessing it. So what could I say?

I motioned to Drake to step out on the porch. I needed to know for sure how much he was to be paid. He pompously sauntered out the white wrought-iron door behind me. When we were out of Lucille's earshot, I asked, "So you and Aunt Lucille agreed on six hundred, right?"

"No, six fifty," he blurted.

I thought Lucille couldn't hear us, but she called out, "I don't remember no conversation about six fifty."

"Six fifty!"

I had no choice but to let it go at that. There was no time to find anyone else, and Lucille needed someone there with her. The memory of her falling in the bathtub made the decision for me. I hoped this was not a sign of things to come.

We walked back inside, and Drake stalked to the rear of the house. Lucille pulled the sweater tight over her chest.

"Auntie, you're to pay Drake six hundred fifty dollars a month. He says that's what you all agreed upon."

"And he won't be paying for nothin?"

"I guess not," I shrugged.

At that point, she agreed. Maybe it was because she was caught between the proverbial

rock and a hard place.

"He wants to be paid one hundred and sixty-two dollars weekly. You will pay for food, utilities and maintaining the household."

Drake must have thought he had me and Lucille over a barrel. He stormed out to his truck and returned with a few plastic bags and an armful of clothes. I wondered where all of his belongings were. I didn't see even a suitcase, a bed, or a chest of drawers. Were all of his worldly possessions balled up in a few plastic bags? A grown man? Surely that wasn't all of it.

Now Drake had moved in with Lucille.

I inched close to Lucille and whispered, "Bye, I'll see you."

Lucille perked up. "When you coming back?"

"Maybe tomorrow." Even though I wasn't at ease, I hoped to put her at ease. "Maybe tomorrow."

Chapter 7

On July 1, I found myself speeding to Lucille's house for the appointment with the Adult Care Action Network (ACAN) representative. The meeting was set for 1:30 that afternoon, and it was already 1:22. When I arrived at the 1950s-style white house with green trim, the chain link fence seemed like a formidable obstacle to reaching the porch. I sat in my car for a moment to collect myself, and to keep from encountering Drake. He was inside, and lately, anytime I came to visit, he would find some way to insult me. I was sick of his "Just do what you gotta do and get outta here" attitude. I had a feeling that this time would be no different. It was supposed to be about Lucille, but Drake always found a way to make it about me.

I scooted out of my car and pushed the gate open. By then I was able to say to myself, "Yeah, I'm here and I'm not leaving until I finish what I came here to do." Then an eerie sick feeling came over me. Pain, weakness, or perhaps both took over. I felt like vomiting. I could actually feel the stress and anxiety. My arthritic knees were screaming and jerking. But I kept moving. I gathered my wits and made it up the steps, gearing up for mental and verbal battle.

I had a key to the house, but out of courtesy, I rang the doorbell. I could see Lucille through the screen door sitting in her favorite green chair. Drake came and unlocked the door. I entered and spoke to him, but he said nothing, not even a mumble. There was nothing pleasant about being around him. Staying home, doing laundry, and taking care of other personal matters would have been a better option. But then there was Lucille, with no one else in the entire world to look into her affairs. She shouldn't have made the final decision to have Drake as a caretaker. A stranger with credentials would have been a better choice, but it was done. Her body and mind had already begun to show that she was making bad decisions. I could see that she was at the point where she needed someone to speak for her. I was the person who had been looking out for her interests for eight years. Now she needed an advocate. Someone to speak for her. Trying to hold onto the strength of her old life and watching her independence slip away were going to be rough pills for Lucille to swallow.

"Danielle," she said, "I just don't know what I would do without you."

I think she said that at the times when she didn't trust Drake. "Drake is all for self and self only." She was on to something, but she just didn't know how ominous that something was. Neither did I, not really. Not to the depth of chicanery I was seeing unfold.

Lucille's house was filled with furniture that defined the mid-1950s. It seemed that her mind had gotten stuck in that time period. Everything in the house transported me back to warm, cozy nights with Amos 'n Andy, plastic slipcovers, and cookies for us when we came to visit. Changing the interior of her house, buying new furniture or pictures was not Lucille's way. She bought one set of furniture, and, according to all accounts, one set was sufficient. She put the "F" back in the word *frugal*. She never squandered a dime. She said her husband had worked too hard for it. All of her family and friends knew that about her.

The 50's Big Band music still played from her record player. Lucille loved music, and music loved Lucille. They were made for each other. Pipe in the music and watch Lucille dance. Back in the day, she had been a free spirit, loving the fun of life.

Her husband Nat had had the distinct honor of being one of the original Pullman Porters on the Southern Pacific Railroad. Nat had lots of character–he was a man of integrity who was deeply in love with Lucille. He spoke about her in glowing terms. Lucille ate up the compliments, as if they were served on Lennox china with Roger's Brother's silver.

Nat traveled extensively for his job, often leaving Lucille at home. But on many occasions when he was leaving for work, she already had her bags packed. According to Lucille, there was no better way to travel than on the train. "You get a real education," She would say.

She told me all the people she had met on her trips and how she had maintained friendships with many of them for years. She collected trinkets. So, anytime she wanted to be transported back in time or place, she would take a seat in the living room and communicate with the memorable place by talking to that particular trinket in her hand. Each one had its own spot on either the coffee table or one of the end tables.

"Now Nat and I arrived at the big Elks Ball that night in St. Louis, Missouri. All the women were in glittering gowns, and all the men were in tuxedos. The Benny Goodman Band was playing. And that's when we stepped in. And Lord a mercy, the band caught fire, and the whole room waved and preened at our grand entrance. That was some night." She kissed the little Elks icon the group bestowed on Nat that night. Then she set it back in its place.

In the early days when we were children, Aunt Lucille would clean and polish each trinket, making sure nothing broke. I remember her saying, "Sit down, and don't touch nothin." So the furniture had survived, with no mishaps, even through the growing years of her nieces and nephews.

Now the air was filled with tension. It was so thick you could cut it with a knife. Lucille looked up and saw me. Her face lit up like a Christmas tree.

"How are you, Lucille?" I sang.

"Danielle, you just don't know what I'm going through."

"I won't know if you don't tell me."

She looked around the corner and hesitated, then sighed with what I took to be depression and confusion, almost like she wanted to give up.

Lucille's lifestyle and habits were usually like a road map. You could set your watch by Lucille's daily habits--they were like clockwork. But lately, she had been getting up between one and two o'clock every afternoon. She had always been an early riser, getting up about 7:30 in the morning. By 9:00 o'clock, she was eating her breakfast. Then she cleaned her kitchen and prepared to take her daily walk. There was a time when she walked about four miles a day until her knees started hurting. So, instead, she would walk the long walkway on her property.

"Danielle, you know, I miss the long walks I used to have with Nat," she would say.

Around noon, Lucille would eat her lunch, and by 12:30, she'd take her afternoon nap. Naptime was over at 1:30, not a minute later. She would get up and often listen to her back-in-the-day transistor radio. Lucille loved news radio. She has to be one of only a few to still have one of those transistor radio gems. By mid-afternoon, Lucille was preparing her dinner. Healthy eating came naturally for her. "I'm eating some baked fish, some carrots, and some cabbage, and, oh yeah, I made me some cornbread. Come and get some."

The way she described that food, it took on a life of its own. Lucille loved to cook for herself. But now, she had clearly lost her routine and her strength to cook, even though she protested that she could still do it.

Since Drake had come, he slept in the extra bedroom next to hers. When Lucille went to her bedroom, she had to go past the pigsty Drake had set up. He was always watching TV, day and night. That annoyed her. Just passing that room upset her.

"Nat would turn over in his grave if he saw this," she would say. They had lived with a place for everything and everything in its place.

Now, Drake didn't get up every day and make his bed, let alone organize his space.

What she failed to realize was, according to Drake, "If you're not getting out of bed, or getting out for only a short time, what's the need in making it up?"

"What's he mean leaving the bed unmade all day long?" she whispered to me. "That's room done become a big old trashcan." She seemed to feel helpless in caring for her things.

Lucille sniffled, and began to cry.

"What's the matter, Lucille?"

"I just walked in my own kitchen. And lo and behold, the dishes wasn't washed. I just asked him why he hadn't washed his dishes, and he said, 'I save 'em up and wash 'em all at once.'"

Lucille wiped her eyes. "You know you can tell a good woman by the way she keeps her kitchen and her bathroom. I walked to the sink and washed the dishes, thinking he ought to be shamed of hisself."

What Lucille didn't know was that Drake had left dirty dishes in the sink wherever he lived and with whomever he lived. And her asking him about it disturbed him, undoubtedly. She was making noise during his TV time.

"He screamed at me, 'Get your old ass outta here, right now.'" Lucille looked around. "That scared me. I was weak in my knees, so I grabbed my walker to steady myself." Lucille realized she was whispering too loud and lowered her voice.

I imagined her feeling like a wounded child with nowhere to go and nobody to rescue her. The ACAN representative interrupted Lucille's disturbing revelation. After some introductory remarks, she moved right into asking Lucille questions that would get her set up for someone to come and help bathe her, take her to the doctor, and send her Meals-On-Wheels. I answered the questions that involved Lucille's affairs outside of her home. I called Drake in to answer questions about things happening inside Lucille's home.

"I'm here, so Lucille don't want no ACAN," Drake yelled.

The ACAN representative looked frightened. "And you're the caretaker in the home?" she asked.

"You damn right," Drake boasted.

The representative gathered her papers, and with a few nebulous comments promptly left.

My mind went back swiftly to an incident when Drake had been living with Lucille for only a few days. He told me he was going out of town and I needed to find someone to stay with Lucille.

"You're leaving when?" I asked.

"Monday."

"You mean, like tomorrow?" I exclaimed.

"Yeah."

"You've got to be kidding. You're giving me eight hours to find someone to come and stay with her?"

"You heard me."

"I don't believe you. How long are you going to be gone?"

"Till Wednesday."

The thoughts I had about Drake right then weren't good–not at all! That man, who had promised to care for his aunt, for pay, had done another low-down thing. Lucille got caught in the cross-fire of his anger towards me.

I left immediately because I didn't have much time to find someone. I called a number of different home health agencies. Each one told me about the last-minute fees I would incur. But I needed somebody in a hurry. I was at their mercy and agreed to the fees.

Drake always claimed that Lucille didn't want strangers in her house, and there was no need for strangers in her house. Well, the "strange" lady from the agency showed up as agreed, and Lucille loved her. All went well. So much for that false statement.

Two weeks later, I had scheduled another ACAN visit. The representative asked to see the bottles of medications Lucille was taking. Drake stormed out, and then came back with Lucille's medicine bottles. He shoved the nine bottles of medicine at the representative, and they fell to the floor. As the lady bent down to pick them up, Drake stood there looking smug.

I was seething from humiliation. How dare he make a scene like that? But evil and ignorance make themselves seen at the most inopportune moments. My need to stay was greater than my desire to leave Lucille alone. I stayed.

"Are you okay?" I asked the representative.

She could sense my embarrassment.

"Are you okay?" she asked.

"I apologize."

The ACAN representative explained how the program worked. She advised me that it would take approximately thirty days to evaluate Lucille's application. We would be notified by mail. The appointment was over, and so was my need to be at Lucille's house. I was never so desperate to get out of a place! Did I forget anything? I didn't think so.

As I was leaving, I could hear my cousin's voice saying, "Danielle, be sure to gather all of Lucille's personal papers before you leave and take them to your house." Now I'm glad I listened.

Before leaving, I walked into the bathroom and took a look at her sleeping pill bottles. "Take as needed," was written on them. One bottle was empty after 24 days? No wonder Lucille looked confused all the time. She looked as if Drake had locked her away and she had little or no contact with the outside world.

Chapter 8

July 9, 2004: Dear God, give me more strength. My body is feeling weak as the days go by... Danielle sat and wrote carefully in her diary.

I had just returned from vacation in Atlanta, and the July sun was already shining hot at 12 o'clock when I walked into Lucille's house. The wonderful relaxed feeling from being on vacation was immediately replaced with the disgusting feeling of being in the same house with Drake. My burden returned. Just thinking about Lucille's situation was a weight I felt hard-pressed to bear.

I took a deep breath and sighed, not from relief but from resignation for what I was about to face. I walked that familiar walkway and mounted the steps. I had already had my person-to-person conversation, and reminded myself that confronting Drake was going to be another trauma.

When I entered the house, Lucille was sitting in her favorite green chair. She invited me to sit on the mauve plastic-covered chair. Anybody visiting Lucille was relegated to sitting in that chair. I could make a big deal about sitting somewhere else, but for what? No one questioned her about sitting in the chair. Everybody just took a seat in that half-moon 1950s-style plastic-covered chair. But today, it was burning up outside and the hot plastic stuck to my legs. In a few minutes, I could feel my legs sweating.

Drake stormed out and into the rear of the house. Lucille smiled, almost like a child wanting to tell a secret. "Danielle, I'm so glad to see you. I got something to tell you."

I could hardly wait. It wasn't that I didn't appreciate her hearty welcome, but I had to wonder what surprise lay behind that glowing face today.

"Lucille, you look wonderful. How are you feeling today?"

She shook her head without a word. "That Drake. That boy is so lazy you'd think he was dead."

I could see that he wasn't doing anything for her. Her hair wasn't combed. Her clothes were falling off her thin, fair shoulders. I rummaged through her closet and changed her pants and that awful top she was wearing. The outfit she had been wearing looked like someone had just grabbed something without looking and said, "Here, put this on." Her socks should have been trashed long ago. I changed them. She sat there looking, perhaps wondering what in the world was happening to her.

Drake stormed back in the room where we were sitting. "You're going to have to change Lucille's bank." Not hi. Not hello. Or, how are you? Just a demand.

I thought about what he said and became indignant at the same time. "For what?"

Lucille had done her banking at this one branch for more than 50 years, and it was as if she had made some sort of commitment to stay with the institution. This demand of Drake's didn't sound one bit like Lucille.

She understood exactly what Drake was saying. She bolted from her chair and, with both crassness and indignation, let him have it.

"You not changing my bank." As if her voice was doing a modulation on a musical scale, she clearly made her position known. "You change your own bank." That was a big step toward standing up to Drake, and she did it! Lucille seemed agitated by the notion of changing the place where she had done business for so many years. Just the fact that Lucille stood her ground with Drake was a miracle. I was proud of her.

"Why does she need to change her bank?" I asked Drake.

"While you were on your vacation, I wrote a check for six hundred dollars—"

Don't tell me I heard what I thought I heard. I could have competed in the Olympics and won Gold with the flips and somersaults my mind did. I couldn't believe what I had heard. Tell me it ain't so.

He continued. "When I gave it to the teller, he wouldn't cash it."

"So what happened?" I asked.

"I went out to the truck and brought her into the bank to authorize the check."

I guarantee Lucille had no idea what she authorized. Lucille had done business with this bank for more than 50 years and there were employees there who knew her and, obviously, someone became concerned about this $600 check. All of that was out-of-character for Lucille. She rarely went into the bank. Her banking was done through direct deposits. The teller told Drake his identification wasn't sufficient.

"I didn't give Drake permission to cash no check," Lucille said.

It's a good thing I was sitting down. I felt dizzy. I couldn't believe it. My thoughts were coming faster than I could sort them out. They were running through my mind like spontaneous combustion. My first thought was, why did Drake need to cash Lucille's check for any amount? Before I left for vacation, I made sure all of Lucille's outstanding bills were paid. Drake had been paid, and I even left cash for her to use.

My next question was, where did he find a blank check? Lucille's checks were among the personal property that I had taken to my home for safekeeping. There were too many questions. I became suspicious that Drake was angry not just with me, he was angry with the world. I now believed he was capable of taking advantage of his father's dear sister.

"Where did you get her check?"

"In the house."

I reeled from that news. I was not satisfied with the flimsy answer Drake gave regarding the check. And, as if it was okay to move on, he swept aside my questions about the check and went on talking about a bed. I could hardly understand his mumbling. Were his scrambled words intentional? I might not have known anything about a bed, but Lucille chimed in and made it clear.

"I ain't buying no bed." Drake must have tried to convince her to buy him a new bed before I arrived. "The one you sleeping on is good enough," Lucille argued.

Will the desires of one aging person have to give in to greed? I wondered.

A few short weeks later, when I visited Lucille, she was sitting in her favorite seat, seemingly in a state of wonder. I went to the dining room and saw Drake sleeping on a very expensive Tempur-Pedic bed. He had done it. In his state of delusion, he had convinced himself that Lucille wanted him to have the bed and that's why she purchased it. The sofa bed that Drake had been sleeping on was no longer good enough. He had tossed it into the back yard for the cats to sleep on. I knew I had to do something drastic.

Chapter 9

Danielle sat on the edge of the sink in the bathroom, writing in her diary.

July 10, 2004:   Dear God, I think the only thing I need now is strength to carry me through this. Here is the latest thing that happened...

My phone rang, and it was Lucille. I detected something strange about her call. First of all, after the bathtub incident, Lucille hadn't dialed my phone number. Did I need to go into crisis mode now? No, I told myself, she just wants to talk with me.

Lucille sounded very direct and focused, as if she had just concluded some mental drilling and had been ordered to call me. She reminded me of a puppet.

"Danielle, I want you to bring me my living trust?"

That question knocked me off my feet. I tried to steady myself because I felt like I was losing it. I got in gear real fast. Something was wrong. What could she want with her living trust? Or, even worse, who would care about her living trust? She had that trust drawn up on October 12, 2000, and, frankly, it was nobody's business what was in it.

Right then, I offered a prayer of gratitude to God for giving me the presence of mind to take Lucille's living trust out of her house before I went to Atlanta. That was my first step of doing something drastic to protect Lucille. Then my detective juices started flowing, and I began to put two and two together. Drake had been pressuring Lucille about her personal papers, and Lucille had evidently told Drake that I had taken the papers to my house.

"Lucille, what do you want with your living trust?" I asked.

Lucille was just like an actor who couldn't remember her lines. The unprepared actor is always looking for a cue to jog her memory. This untrained actor turned her head away from the phone and said, "She wants to know what I want with my living trust."

"Tell her because it's yours," the voice said.

"I want it because it's mine," she said.

I wondered how long they had practiced. Seemingly not long enough. You've got to get up earlier than that to fool me. Who do they think I am? Drake was telling Lucille what to say, and she was repeating his promptings. Lucille was 87, and her mind was just like the weather. On any given day, one never knew if the sun would be shining or whether rain would come.

"Lucille, I'm not bringing you your living trust," I said.

"Okay," she said in a low monotone.

I was past annoyed and hung up the phone. What more was there to talk about? I would get to the bottom of it.

* * *

July 11, 2004: I arrived at Lucille's house, only to face what had become too common an occurrence. I was preparing myself.

I knew Drake was going to be Drake, and the very thought of it made me sick. My stress level was going through the roof. I mounted the steps and dragged myself to the door. Lucille was sitting in that green chair looking out the window.

"Hi, Lucille."

"Hi, sweet girl." She gave me the biggest smile.

Drake turned and stalked out of the room. The minute he was gone, I moved close to Lucille. "Don't ask me to bring you any of your personal papers anymore. They're safe with me. You know they are."

In a hushed tone, as if trying to hide her words from Drake, Lucille whispered, "That's right, you keep everything. Don't bring me nothin."

"Okay."

Her mind always seemed to be struggling for a breakthrough. But this time, she was successful. When she told me to keep everything, I knew she knew what she was saying. In that moment of clarity, she knew her papers were safe with me.

Chapter 10

July 24, 2004: As usual, I arrived early to check on Lucille, to make sure she was okay. She was my number-one priority. My visits always brought great comfort to her. Lately, though, she seemed not to notice. Every time I went to see her, she was groggy. I asked myself, what in the world is going on. If her look of despair and discouragement captured exactly what Lucille was going through, it wasn't good. It was a perfect moment of doom and gloom. She looked doped up. She could hardly function. How many of those sleeping pills–or, better yet, those "death" pills–was she taking?

When she spoke, she didn't seem to recognize me. Out of concern, I asked her, "Lucille, why can't you hold your head up?" I didn't want to tell her it was drooping to the side. "Are you tired?"

"I don't know."

"How do you feel?"

"I don't feel good."

"What hurts you?"

"I don't know. I just don't feel good."

Lucille sat quietly in that favorite green chair. Let me tell you, whoever made Lucille's green chair deserved a merit for durability of workmanship. She had been sitting in that same chair for as long as I am old, and it was still meeting her needs.

I had to find some distraction to think about, and the green chair was as good as anything, I guessed.

The way she looked that day, anybody could have come into her house and walked right past the chair without her knowing it. For some reason, she looked particularly unhappy. There was a cloud hovering over and swirling around her. She didn't try to hide it. She didn't know how. My mind ran fast because I was looking at a woman who was okay a few weeks ago, but in just a few days had sunk into the depths of despair.

Okay, granted, before she went into the hospital, she was beginning to show some normal signs of aging, but since being home with Drake, she had taken a deep plunge downward, like falling from the highest peak of Mt. Shasta. She seemed to be saying she wanted out. Drake had been living with her for only about a month.

Lucille finally raised her head and started to talk.

"What's wrong?" I asked.

"My house is not my house no mo?"

"What do you mean your house isn't your house anymore?"

"I can't do nothin' in my own house."

"What do you mean?"

"Since Drake come to live with me, I can't do nothin." She peered around the corner from her seat. "Look at that nasty room. Nat is turning over in his grave."

"Is that the problem?"

"Drake. Everything was good till he come. Now, I can't say nothin' or do nothin' in my own house. Now, you know that's a shame."

Although I nodded, I was still concerned. Lord, what am I going to do? "Auntie, assisted living is good. Don't you want to—"

"I'm just a prisoner. A prisoner in my own house." Lucille knew she couldn't live alone anymore, but she refused to discuss assisted living.

I wondered if I shouldn't use my advocacy powers and take her to a facility. I sighed. As long as that person, my beloved aunt, had a will, she shouldn't be taken against her will. I wasn't sure if that was the right answer anymore. And yet, Lucille was facing more than she could ever have imagined, and she was helpless to do anything about it. I was her advocate. I asked myself if I was doing right or wrong. Wasn't she supposed to be gaining something by having someone living with her? On those long hot days of summer, anything Drake said or did annoyed her. She knew he had to stay, or she would have to go to assisted living. That still didn't make her like her present situation, not one bit!

* * *

July 25, 2004: Drake asked me to get Lucille's prescription refilled. I couldn't look at him when I took the medicine card. I just took it without comment. I could still see her groggy, inattentive, incoherent, and suffering look from severe alterations in her sleep pattern. She was averaging one sleeping pill per day. It was obvious her 87-year-old system couldn't process that amount of medication. To give her that many sleeping pills in a month was unconscionable. I called her doctor about it, and he asked that Lucille's caretaker give him a call. So I asked Drake to call the doctor and give him a report on the medication Lucille was taking.

Anyone who knows Lucille will say she is an example, even if she doesn't know it, of the maxim in Benjamin Franklin's Poor *Richard's Almanac*, "Early to bed and early to rise makes a man *(woman)* healthy, wealthy and wise." Lucille believed in getting her rest. According to Lucille, a good night's sleep and a nap everyday was the way to go. She didn't need an alarm clock. Her built-in one had always served her well. So, honestly, it is beyond anyone's comprehension that Lucille would need to take an entire bottle of sleeping pills in a month. I became increasingly anxious about what toll this medication was taking on her, both mentally and physically. But after a full month, Drake never reported back about calling the doctor.

I started making pop calls on Lucille and found her getting up between noon and one o'clock in the afternoon. Even with the assistance of her walker, she swayed a lot when she walked. It was sad watching her, and it was obvious that the sleeping pills were taking a toll on her. I would call and cancel them altogether.

On my latest visit, I didn't see a woman full of life with interesting conversation. I saw an elderly woman who was a mere shell of her old self. She was unkempt, disheveled, and looked as if she had no clue where she was. She was having difficulty keeping her eyes open. "Can I go lay down?" she often asked. Lucille obviously knew what she felt wasn't normal. "Am I taking too much sleep medicine?" she asked.

I was thinking that anyone with a shred of smarts wouldn't continue giving Lucille medication she couldn't tolerate. But then I thought of Drake. To have Lucille "out" with sleep medication would give Drake an opportunity to do even less for her. He could watch his TV programs 24/7 without interruption. He wouldn't have to prepare breakfast and lunch because Lucille was now getting up at 1 in the afternoon. He had to prepare only dinner. But he was hired to prepare meals three times a day. Then I remembered that Drake had told me, in one of his delusional moments, that he felt entitled to the money Lucille paid him, without any of the services. Come on, I thought, this was a lady who, up until very recently, had been doing everything for herself. Now she couldn't do anything because she was being drugged out. There has to be a law for elderly abuse somewhere, I pondered.

Now Lucille reached over and posed a question. "Drake, I can't find my safe deposit box key."

"What?" Now that was pure trouble in her present situation, with Drake in the house.

Chapter 11

When I drove away from Lucille's home, I was more worried than ever. Thoughts of her unknowingly telling Drake that the key to her safe deposit box was lost meant the gravest problem. I thought to myself, if she tells him, he'll go after the box. But who was I fooling? Lucille was in the house with Drake, and she got lonely because he was always watching TV or sleeping. And, when little snippets of conversation took place during T.V. commercials, she convinced herself that it was okay to tell him everything. Each day ushered in the need for a new tactic with Drake, depending on what he wanted. Lucille didn't have the ability to match his deceit.

Under normal circumstances, it would seem better if Lucille did not talk with him at all, but she wasn't able to make such decisions. On those occasions when she was mentally clear, she could stand her ground with Drake. But those times were becoming less and less frequent.

I wondered what old people want out of life when they reach Lucille's age. One day, I asked Lucille that question.

"Cook my food, clean my house, and make sure you take care of me," she answered.

I interpreted that to mean she wanted to feel safe. Was that too much to ask? Was it out of the realm of possibilities? I tried to assess how much safety she had. Well, when she was sleeping until 1 or 2 in the afternoon, and then got up for the day, it was almost time for her to have her dinner and go back to bed. She looked worn, hardly able to function.

I recalled Lucille talking about her younger years as a strong woman. She grew up in Texas, the second child among 7. With that many brothers and sisters, if nothing else, she knew how to fight for her rightful position in the family. She had to be sharp and always alert. If not, she would have been left out of her mother's homemade ice cream.

All of the older folks said Lucille was a beautiful child. You can't tell such children much, because they feel invincible. That's exactly who Lucille was. Free. Running and chasing, jumping and skipping, playing baseball, and throwing balls against walls. She rode merry-go-rounds, played tetherball for hours on end, and ran around schoolyards, for what seemed like never-ending hours. She was vibrant and admired.

Lucille never had many things to worry about. Her father and mother never allowed her to lack for anything. When she married Nat, he did the same, and he left her well cared for, with cash in a safe deposit box, cash in both of her accounts, a home, and insurance. She had lived past her three score and ten years that the Bible promised, and she never wanted for anything. She lived a simple life and took care of all that she had. Miss Frugality was her pet name. She cherished each day as a blessing from God.

She wanted to be safe? Why can't she have this? I asked myself. Is this asking too much? Why couldn't she feel safe in the home in which she had lived for so long? Drake was the only one who could answer that question, but I dared not ask him.

Lucille desperately scrambled to bring thoughts together in some sort of order. When I talked with her, she reached into thin air, trying to come up with answers. When she wasn't sleeping, she was trying to block the negative effects of the sleeping pills.

That seemed to annoy Drake beyond reasonableness. It infringed upon his time. Well, he was paid to give Lucille his time. What was she paying him for? More and more, I found myself trying to answer that question. More and more, I found myself asking how I could break the unthinkable cycle of things happening to Lucille and to the family. That was a heart-pounding question that I still couldn't answer.

Chapter 12

August 3, 2004: Dear God, life is sinking me deeper and deeper every day into depression, or a sense of helplessness. I need guidance. Help me to see my duty in this impossible situation.... Danielle continued to write.

The mid-morning sunshine was bright and strong. I had so many things to do, but everything had to wait because I had promised Lucille I would come by that day. Since I had made her the promise, I felt it was my duty to keep it; otherwise, she would look at me strange when I did visit.

When I arrived at Lucille's house, we went through our usual greeting routine, and I went about taking care of paying her utility bills. When I finished, I told her, "I'm going now."

"When you coming back?" she asked, as was her regular routine.

Trying to be truthful, but at the same time giving myself a little room to tend to personal matters, I answered, "Probably in a day or two."

"Okay."

She always seemed to be okay with that, as long as she felt I was coming back. There was something about my coming back that made her feel comfortable. It was sort of like her cooking and eating boiled cabbage and carrots and baked fish. They satisfied her. That was a good meal. My visits satisfied her.

But when I left, I felt ill at ease. Something that I could not see on the surface wasn't right. Something was out of balance.

* * *

Lately, any time I visited Lucille's house, Drake was in a foul mood. Two days later, when I left my home to return to her house, the dread of encountering Drake made me feel sick. The stress was overwhelming. It was becoming more and more of a task to go to Lucille's house. I'd avoid her house like the plague if I could. I pulled myself together by blocking the conversation with myself: Just stay home. You don't have to endure that. But I promised her I would be back. I had to see with my own eyes that Lucille was okay.

The last time I was there, I had an overwhelming feeling that she was in danger. What secret emotional and psychological damage was being inflicted on her that not even I could detect? Lucille was a prime target for unscrupulous people.

As badly as I was feeling with all the nausea, tension headaches, and downright I'm-sick-of-you-Drake ailments, I decided to go. I got to Lucille's porch and picked up her mail. Now I would brave the inside and bathe and dress her. Drake was there like acne on your backside. You know it's there, but you can't get rid of it.

I rang the doorbell and waited for Drake to unlock the door. The minute I stepped inside, Drake yelled at me. "Damn! You can't wait till you're asked to come here?"

"Drake, I didn't come here for any of your mess." I walked past him.

"My mess! You the only mess I know. Comin' over here bothering a woman who don't want to be bothered with you."

Today Drake was in a foul mood. His attitude was putrid. I wonder why he couldn't smell it.

"Get your old ass out of here."

"Well, I just arrived to see my aunt."

"You deserve to be dead."

"This is not your house and you can't tell me to get out." I started looking for Lucille. She was sitting alone in her bedroom.

Drake followed me, cursing and threatening. Lucille couldn't stand to look up at him. I thought it was her way of being embarrassed. The last time I tried to talk to my mother about Drake, she said she was praying for him. Now Lucille was looking off to the side with that stroke-looking droop to her head. Drake's attitude must have turned it to the side. It struck me as what he wanted.

"Nothing would please you more than for me to stop visiting Lucille. Not on your life, buddy. No way."

I started to take her to the bathroom to bathe her. When I looked at her, I was reminded of an abducted child, finally rescued. Lately, every time I saw her, she was complaining about Drake, something he was or was not doing. This time was no exception. In the bathroom, as I washed her frail body, she complained about Drake's filthy room.

"Did you see that dirty room? Nat is turning over in his grave. Drake oughta be ashamed of hisself."

"Did you tell him that?" I wiped the bath water from her body with a towel.

"It don't do no good."

At least while I was here, she was safe. I felt pure animosity for Drake. I tried hard to ignore him, and to forgive him, but he kept opening the wound every time I came to visit Lucille. And today was no different. Angry thoughts swirled in my head because as I dried Lucille, Drake was cursing me.

"See. There you go. Meddling. Taking over my job."

"If you ever did your job, I wouldn't have to be meddling, or taking over. Don't you think?"

"Get out!"

"You're just a hired hand, so how can you tell me to get out?"

My stomach tightened like a newly woven ball of yarn. I thought to myself, this can't be worth it, can it? I don't know if he was more enraged with me because of what I said or because he had been found out. Either way, it didn't make him look very good. Well, since he wasn't acting out his nephew role, he was definitely no more than a "hired hand." Even if this job had promotional opportunities, he had disqualified himself.

At that stage of Drake's ranting, I wrapped Lucille in a big towel, and Drake headed back to his room. Lucille dressed and moved toward the living room, using the hallway wall to assist her. Midway down the hallway, she abruptly stopped. Walking behind her, I couldn't see any reason why she stopped. She turned toward me while leaning against the wall for balance.

"Danielle, did Drake tell you to get outta my house?"

"Yes."

"He can't tell you to get outta my house. This is my house."

I didn't know if her statement was based on what Drake had said to me earlier in the day, or if it was something she'd been trying to knit together in her mind from other times Drake had told me to get out. But, then, it really didn't matter. Lucille had said it, and that was that. She proceeded down the hallway and into the living room, where she sat down in her favorite green folding chair.

Lucille sat and stared out the 1950s-style wood-framed picture window. Her look was that of a blank check drawn on a closed account. I realized that I would have no meaningful conversation with her, as much as I had hoped that we would. Lucille was in a state of bewilderment. She had been thrust into the unenviable position of having to choose sides. She said nothing to Drake.

"Lucille, do you want me to get out of your house?" I asked.

That question put her in an uncompromising position. I needed to know. I needed to know if Drake was speaking out of an assumed position of authority, or whether Lucille had given him authority to speak for her.

"Do you want me to leave?"

In one of her most lucid and precise statements in a long time, Lucille said, "No. Who said I did?"

Drake's demand for me to leave came from one of his delusional moments of authority. Now we both knew where we stood while she was in a rational state of mind.

Chapter 13

I called a meeting of family to discuss what I was going through with Drake and Lucille. I couldn't manage to get them together for one reason or the other, so I set up a phone meeting.

I defined what I knew of the relationship between Drake and Lucille. "We need to do something, and I want your honest opinion."

Liz, my sister who lives in Atlanta, said that she would abide by my decision because I was the one saddled with Lucille's day-to-day care.

My sister Brenda said, "I can't do anything against my blood brother. I pray that he gets saved and goes to heaven."

My mother refused to have any input against her son.

When I hung up, I felt alone. Totally and devastatingly alone. Who was going to stand by me? If I made a move against Drake, I was going to lose my family. I could see it sticking out like a blade out of a rock. I didn't know what to say to myself, or for myself. I went to bed wearier than I could imagine.

* * *

Lucille made the biggest mistake of her life when she asked Drake if he knew where the key to her safe deposit box was. I started worrying that she had set off a search for her key. I wondered if Drake would ask me for the key. It had been well over a week since she had asked him, and he hadn't asked me a thing. Maybe that was a good thing. But why not mention the missing key to me, since I handled her business affairs? I should have known that he had no intention of acknowledging me as the person Lucille trusted, as the person who had been taking care of her affairs for eight years without touching a dime. He wanted to take care of all her business affairs.

Lucille always said, "He can't take care of his own affairs."

She had suffered a serious lapse in memory when she mentioned the key to Drake. Lucille's question to Drake about the key provided no answer, but his devious mind must have gone into high gear. He must have tried to figure out how to handle the question without involving me. Ralph Waldo Emerson said it best, "What you do speaks so loud that I cannot hear what you say."

Character and integrity were not what this man was at all about. The Emerson phrase spoke loudly of just who he was. I believe with all my heart, though, that "What's done in the dark shall be revealed in the light."

* * *

August 14, 2004: I drove to Lucille's bank. I was so elated to go there and make her finances safe. I told myself to calm down, but I was too nervous and anxious. All I wanted to do was to make sure the safe deposit box hadn't been tampered with. Then I would be relieved. I would know for sure that her money and personal property were safe. "Today I'll be assured!" I thought.

I paused and looked for the window servicing the safe deposit boxes.

"May I help you?" the teller asked.

"I would like to enter Box #3576," I requested.

"Is this your box?"

"No."

"Whose name is on the box?"

"My name is on the box, but the box belongs to Lucille Stanton."

"What's your name?"

"Danielle Carrington."

"Is your name on the card as a signer?"

"Yes."

"If you'll wait here, I'll pull the card."

"Thank you."

The teller pulled Lucille's card with my name on it. The receptionist cleared me to enter the somber area. After a click, I walked behind a huge glass door requiring strength to open. I saw the gun-metal-colored safe deposit boxes along the wall.

The teller climbed a ladder to get Lucille's box, which was at the top. I was nervous and anxious. I watched and wondered when the teller was going to reach Lucille's box. Until I opened the box, I wouldn't know for sure whether or not Drake had gone into it. I just wanted to make sure he had not confiscated anything, including her $70,000 in cash. Hurry, I thought. Why doesn't she rush? Finally! The teller pulled out Lucille's safe deposit box, climbed down, and handed the box to me. Although I didn't know what I would discover after opening the box, I was hopeful. I felt that by having the box in my hands, my anxiety would disappear. I thought, I'll just open the box, examine the contents, and be able to breathe a deep sigh of relief.

I thought of the man who was putting me through all of this anxiety. A man intoxicated with selfishness. A man who had never been able to put anyone else's needs above his own. A man with a narcissistic hangover. I nervously opened the box. Praise God! Thank you, Jesus. Mystery solved. Drake hadn't been there. I rifled through the personal papers and counted $100 bills until I had laid out $70,000 in stacks. I placed the stacks back inside their 1950s-style light brown window envelopes.

Nat and Lucille grew up during the Depression. They didn't have much money when they first married, but Nat -- being the fine gentleman that he was -- worked tirelessly to provide for himself and his special wife, Lucille. Nat treated Lucille as if she was a first-place trophy he had won. I wondered why he left so much money in the safe deposit box. Why didn't he deposit the money in the bank? Lucille said it was 35 years of tips from the dining car of the railroad company he worked for. He was told he didn't have to pay taxes on money he had in a safe deposit box.

The memory of the Depression was still clear in Lucille's mind. She said it was like a bad dream from which she couldn't wake up. She never wanted to be that poor again.

Nat cherished Lucille like a rare gem. He took great care in assuring her safety and financial security. To Nat, this meant that Lucille would never want for anything. He had done an awesome job in making it turn out that way. Once I asked her about spending some of her money on some things she needed.

"Danielle, if all my money is gone, who I'm gonna depend on?"

She was right. She thought she would have no one to take care of her in the event she had no money. Now, anybody who had a problem seeing this amount of money in the safe deposit box and wishing they had it, should never be anywhere near it. All they needed to do is convince themselves they had to have it. Then they had to find a way to get it.

I was worried because Drake always wanted the very best in the worst way. He would get it by any means! I have to get Lucille to the bank to change her box, I thought. Thankfully, everything was in place, including the deed to her house. I sighed with relief.

Lucille's key still hadn't been located the following week. If I thought for one minute that I should mention this to Drake, it wasn't going to happen. I dared not talk to Drake about the key. I thought that if he knew, he would conjure up a scheme to get his hands on Lucille's money.

If Drake ever got his hands on her money, I was sure he would declare that she gave it to him, or something crazy like that. So, there was no way on earth that I wanted to spark any ideas in Drake's devious mind. I knew him. He would work overtime until he found it. I decided to leave him out of the equation.

I started to hyperventilate when I knew I had to hurry and get Lucille to the bank to get her a new box. I thought, I can't tell her what I'm doing for fear she'll tell Drake. She tells him things she doesn't even remember telling him. I needed that safe deposit box key.

Chapter 14

Danielle sat on her bed and wrote in the diary.

August 17, 2004: Dear God, who can I talk to if not you? I am feeling desperate and helpless. Please help me straighten everything out, especially help me find that key....

That early afternoon, Lucille and I were driving to the notary. I couldn't locate the building where the notary said she would be waiting. I started to panic. I didn't know when I would have access to Lucille again.

"Danielle, you just don't know what I'm going through," Lucille was babbling.

"Lucille, I won't know if you don't tell me." I was more concerned with finding the notary, to give us some leverage. Was Lucille trying to tell me something that was playing back in her mind, or was the complaint based on a new occurrence?

"Do you know what Drake done to me?"

"No."

"He hollered at me and cursed me."

"He cursed at you?"

"He hollered at me and cursed me."

"Is that the first time he's hollered at you?"

"I don't know."

"Why did he holler and curse at you, Lucille?"

"I don't know."

"What did you do to make him so mad at you?"

"It was late one night and I was getting ready for bed. I went into the kitchen, and—."

"Why did you go into the kitchen?"

"For some water before I went to bed."

"So, what happened when you got into the kitchen?"

"I see my kitchen real dirty. Pots and pans and dishes all over the place."

"Did that upset you, Lucille?"

"Yeah."

"Why?"

"Cause I don't leave no dirty dishes in my sink. I wash my dishes every night. I likes to keep my kitchen clean."

What Lucille didn't know about Drake's laziness was no new occurrence. It was exactly what he did while living with his mother. According to him, there was no reason for him to change. Nonetheless, Lucille was upset and irritated with Drake. She would never leave her kitchen dirty at night. That was probably what he had been doing every night.

"Lucille, what did you do?"

"I was washing the dishes."

I interrupted her mid-sentence. "Where was Drake when you were in the kitchen?"

"In that back room watching that old T.V. I was washing pots and pans and swishing the water in the sink, and I guess he heard me."

"Did he walk calmly into the kitchen?"

"No, he stormed into the kitchen."

"Was he upset with you because you were washing the dishes?"

"O-o-o-e-e, he was past upset. He was irate."

"What did he say?"

"What you doing in here?"

"And what did you say?"

"I'm washing my dishes. What it look like I'm doing?"

"Get your old ass out of this kitchen. Now!"

"If you'd a done what you was supposed to do, then the dishes would a been washed."

Lucille relayed to me that, while she spoke to Drake, her eyes were drawn to her old O'Keefe & Merritt range with the accordion top, circa 1952. It was covered with grease as thick as the crust on a pan pizza. She shook her head. She liked things in order. Drake was messy. She liked things clean. Drake lived in filth. She began to cry. Wearily, she hobbled to her room and dragged herself into bed.

I had no one to talk this out with, except my husband. I had no one else from whom I could get advice. I was going to have to make a decision. And it had to be soon. In two hours, I drove away from that misery. I drove away wondering how God would help me to fix it. How many more tears would Lucille have to shed? Drake had made a complete mess of her life and her house. I had allowed her to get in harm's way like nothing else I had done. Lucille wanted him out; I wanted him out. Lucille didn't want to leave her house, though, and she knew she couldn't live alone. Drake had convinced her that she couldn't make it without him.

As I drove away, I could still hear our conversation in my head. I asked Lucille, "Why don't you tell him how you feel?"

"You know, you can't tell Drake nothing. He don't listen to nobody."

I shook my head in disbelief because Lucille had never been more right.

"If he don't respect his momma, then who am I?"

If it weren't for Lucille, Drake would have no place to live. He lived in her house. Ate her food. Slept in her bed. Watched her T.V. 24/7. Burned her electricity day and night.

But who was paying him? So, if for no other reason, Lucille deserved his respect.

"If a person can disrespect the person that birthed them into the world, then what you think he'll do to me."

I had to get the Power of Attorney notarized. It was a must. But we drove around an hour and never found the notary's address. Lucille enjoyed being with me as much as I enjoyed having her along. I bought ice cream cones for both of us—chocolate chip for her, black walnut for me. For some reason, the ice cream seemed extra special that day. I enjoyed every lick.

"Umm, uh, this is good, Danielle," Lucille said.

For a moment, my aunt seemed transported to a pleasant place, enjoying being with me and feeling safe. But I knew she wasn't safe, and I still wasn't sure what to do.

Chapter 15

I sat by my phone and dialed Lucille's number, hoping to speak to her but knowing I probably wouldn't.

"Hello."

I was cautious about what I would say to Drake because yesterday, when I was at her house, I was trying to take her to the notary to have the Power of Attorney signed, and I didn't want to throw up any red flags for Drake to knock down. He didn't know about the Power of Attorney signature, and I was going to leave it that way.

"I'm just calling to say I'll pick Lucille up at twelve."

"She's not going," Drake growled.

I felt the threat of a tension headache and felt woozy. But nothing was going to keep me from going over to her house. I got dressed and rushed out, knowing this might be the mother of all conflicts between Drake and me. I prepared to do battle. Who does he think he is?

Normally, I would sit in my car a moment to collect myself. Today, I shifted my car into park and charged along Lucille's all-too-familiar walkway. I must have sprinted to the front door. I didn't ring the doorbell. Instead, I used my own key to unlock the door. I entered, calling for Lucille.

"Lucille." I walked into the kitchen and found Lucille sitting on a stool. "Why did Drake say you couldn't go with me?"

"I don't feel good, Danielle."

"She's not going!" Drake yelled emphatically.

"Why can't she go?" I yelled back.

"Because I said so."

I took a deep breath, and reminded myself to do the biofeedback exercises—think good thoughts. Breathe in good thoughts. Jesus help me. The foul scenery would not leave my mind. Drake stayed true to his low-down ways. They run as wide as a river and as deep as the sea. Why won't he let her go?

It was one o'clock in the afternoon, and Lucille was just getting up for the day. She had not eaten breakfast or lunch. I walked in the kitchen to fix her some oatmeal, and planned to buy her lunch once we went out. In the small L-shaped kitchen with its oversized appliances, I realized I was standing close to the broiler on the stove. Lucille's food was cooking in the broiler, so I didn't have to fix the oatmeal. Drake yanked the broiler open.

"Move!" he yelled.

I felt the heat, and realized he was trying to scare me by almost burning my leg. He was about to burn me without even caring. I jerked out of his way, weighing what was best for Lucille right then. She looked resigned. I thought it best for me to leave and walked out. I had to make a decision about what to do.

* * *

On August 2, 2004, I had had the sleeping pill prescription refilled that Drake gave me on July 25. I was apprehensive about whether or not to give Lucille's sleeping pills to Drake. I weighed my feelings on a moral scale. Look what has happened with the pills. She wasn't that weak and pale before. She had a regular habit of getting up and living her day before. I decided not to give the prescription to Drake. I couldn't. That was against my better judgment, and I wasn't willing to compromise that.

I was beyond feeling uncomfortable about what family, friends, or Drake might think. I was beyond worrying about what might happen to Lucille if I gave Drake the prescription. I needed time to think what to do about Drake living in her house. I needed time to make arrangements for her to be taken to a safe facility. Or, I needed time to find some agency to come to my house to take care of her.

Lucille always believed she couldn't trust anyone, but now she couldn't mentally grasp that she couldn't trust Drake. The mental abilities just weren't there. Maybe it was because Drake wasn't just anyone. He was family. He promised he would take very good care of her. Sadly, she didn't know what Drake's definition of "take very good care of" meant.

Drake was 58 and still living with his mother because he had nowhere else to go. And just before Drake moved in with Lucille, his mother had had a difficult time trying to get him to pay $200 a month in rent. It stood to good reason that the move to Lucille's house was more for Drake's convenience than taking care of Lucille. I imagined his perverted mouth whispering in Lucille's ear, "You know you need me. I'll take care of you."

Drake took it upon himself to contact Lucille's doctor. He reported that he never received the latest prescription of sleeping pills. Drake had never asked me if I had the prescription refilled. Obviously, he didn't want to call attention to himself.

The doctor's office never asked what happened to the prescription that had just been refilled on August 2. Drake had done what was akin to writing a death sentence for Lucille. Without my knowledge, Drake picked up the prescription. It would keep her quiet. I would have to move with all boldness. I had to do something drastic, and fast.

Chapter 16

My feeling for Drake had grown to near disdain. I dreaded going to that house. I dreaded hearing him greet me with foul language. Why did I have to deal with him at all? Why couldn't I get him out of my life? Out of Lucille's life? He constantly shouted at me, and I knew I was no match for his foul language, his arsenal of hate for me.

Now, he was in the "keep Lucille from her" mood. He gave me excuse after excuse. Every excuse in the book was on his tongue, as to why Lucille couldn't go with me—"She's sick. She can't go today. She don't feel good."

Today, I wondered if he suspected something. Did he know about the lost key? I didn't have an "Ah-ha" moment that preceded clarity. I thrust into high gear. I was so anxiety ridden that my heart felt like it was going to jump right out of my chest. I had to get that safe deposit box changed. Lucille and I had to get new keys made. That chore turned out to be a real emergency. It was the next step to her safety. It was not in Drake's nature to be helpful.

I knew one thing for sure. If Drake knew anything about this missing key, Lucille's personal property, including her money, would all be history. Gone in a flash! I have to get the key, I thought. Lucille is not only my aunt, she's my friend. I'll stop at nothing. She has to get a new box with new keys.

I got out of the car and walked inside the bank. I checked the safe deposit box and all of the items inside. Then I left the bank, somewhat relieved that Lucille's money and personal property were safe. I was still concerned about getting Lucille to the bank to get the new box.

Drake didn't know how much money was in the box, but he knew the box existed, and he knew something of value was in it. I imagined him plotting day and night to get the contents of the safe deposit box into his hands. He would talk to himself about having a big payday!

Lucille's downward spiral had come almost suddenly. So why was I jumping through Drake's hoops? I had to get Lucille to the bank notary to have the Power of Attorney signed and executed. We had to get it done. Now. That was the only way I would have the authority to save her.

Chapter 17

September 21, 2004: Dear God, this is going on and on. Can't you just intervene and let me know you're intervening... Danielle kept writing until it turned dark outside.

When I woke up the next morning, I still felt tired, very tired. But that tiredness wasn't going to stop me from taking my one opportunity to drive Lucille to the bank to get her new safe deposit box and keys. It was even more urgent than the power of attorney. This action and this day were going to take a huge load off my mind.

Still, my mind was suffering from severe fatigue. I couldn't think straight. Most nights, I couldn't sleep. I woke up at 3:00 in the morning and couldn't get back to sleep. I had to snap out of my problems and take care of business.

I didn't have to call Lucille because when I last left her house, I let her know I would be coming on Tuesday to take care of some business. I didn't tell her the nature of the business. Neither did I inform her of the importance of the business. It was information she didn't need to know. That way, I didn't have to worry about her mistakenly telling Drake. I did it for her best interest. Every person Lucille's age should have at least one person they can trust and depend on to help them navigate through the balance of their lives. It had become a daunting task for me. But, I was going to be there for her. Although I've never said it to her, I pledged full allegiance to her in whatever circumstances might arise. She deserved to be protected!

Thoughts of getting her to the bank on the 21st overwhelmed me. I couldn't believe how emotional I had become over the matter. But the day had finally come.

I picked up Lucille without having to see Drake. I guess he figured he couldn't keep her imprisoned for the rest of her days. So he decided not to show his face.

I drove to the bank to get that new safe deposit box and the new set of keys. I held Lucille's arm as we walked and assisted her to a seat. Then I walked to the safe deposit box window and asked the bank manager to allow us to enter. She asked for the primary account holder's name, which I gave her. The manager turned her back and rifled through the file. Then she walked to another file. I walked to the next window closer to where she was and asked whether there was a problem. The manager looked at me strangely. Something was going on.

"The customer came in yesterday, September 20, and requested that her safe deposit box be closed. A man brought her into the bank to do the transaction. He signed his name Drake Black. He took everything."

"He took the deed to her house?"

He had her personal pieces of correspondence and her money—everything gone! I felt sick. Stunned. "Are you sure?"

She reached over and showed me a copy of the transaction for closing Lucille's safe deposit box.

"Isn't that improper?" I asked.

"As long as the box holder was with him." She shrugged.

There should be a law. Anyone with any sense would know that Lucille didn't have a clue about any of this. I gathered myself and made slow but very deliberate steps to where Lucille was sitting. My heart beat at the thought of having to tell her what happened.

"Drake closed the box and took the money," I said in monotone.

Lucille wept. "Can you get my money back?"

"I'll try." What else could I say?

"Where were you when Drake was emptying your safe deposit box? Were you in the booth with him?" I wanted to ask her this, but I knew she didn't know. Now what was my next move? I had been pushed beyond the point of discussing this disaster with the family, and trying to talk sense into Drake's head. I had to make a more definitive move.

Chapter 18

In addition to going to the bank today, Lucille and I had to get the long-awaited Power of Attorney signed and notarized. As my thoughts were going crazy, Lucille just stared at me.

"We have to leave now," I said.

"Where we goin'?"

I didn't actually ignore her, but I didn't answer her because a million thoughts were still swirling around in my head. I knew one answer from me would lead to another question from her. This was not the time to engage in back and forth volleying of questions.

"I don't know where we're going," I said.

So, I made the decision, as long as she wasn't going home right now, that it was okay to delay answering her. With a little assistance from me, she made her way to the door. I followed close behind, ensuring that she was walking with her trusty two-legged walker. How strange! I felt dejection and an incredible sadness coming from the space. We walked cautiously to the car.

As we drove to the notary in Los Angeles, I preferred not to have any conversation with Lucille. But I reminded myself that Lucille couldn't shut down on me. I had to let her talk. She just might remember something about what had happened with Drake at the bank.

"Lucille, do you know that Drake took all the money in your safe deposit box?"

"He did?" She paused. "You gonna get my money back?"

I was hoping the conversation would jolt her mind and she would remember something about that horrible day. I continued talking.

"You gonna get my money back?" She was fixated on my getting her money back. I wondered whether she knew what a monumental task that would be.

"I'll try." What else could I say?

The notary's office was located approximately five miles from the bank, and we were about to reach her office. Rather than allow Lucille to continue to ask questions to which I really had no concrete answer, I decided to focus on something else. I began to feed her questions to ask Drake when she got home.

"Lucille, ask Drake where he put your money." We went over that five times.

I had become somewhat accustomed to Lucille's throwing a statement at me when I had no idea of its origin or its intended target.

She asked, in a can-you-help-me tone, "Danielle, you just don't know what I'm going through?"

"Lucille, I won't know if you don't tell me." That was my constant answer to her continuous complaint.

"My house is not my home no more since Drake moved in."

I'd heard that many times before. I knew it bothered her, but it wasn't about her house right now. I knew that whenever I had occasion to take her somewhere, she seemed to be in a joyful world. But when she said "my home," sadness covered her face. She was sad about Drake ruling her home. She didn't, however, seem to recall the loss of her money right then.

I parked a short distance from the notary's office. Lucille didn't have to walk far. Thankfully, the office wasn't busy, which meant we could see the notary soon. For that I was very grateful. I was still reeling from the safe deposit box scheme when we checked into the front desk.

When our names were called, Lucille managed to get up with my assistance, and we made our way into the notary's office. Lucille was actually the person with whom the notary spoke, but she was unable to answer the notary's questions.

"Huh?" she asked.

I was literally caught up in my emotions, not wanting to do any of this because I was becoming ill and the questions from the notary just took more of my energy. But the need for me to engage in the conversation was more valuable than I would know at the time. Finally, the notary produced the document that gave me Lucille's Power of Attorney.

By the time we left the notary, I had worked up an appetite. Although I was hungry, I could have easily skipped eating. There were more important things to do. However, Lucille needed to eat, so I stopped at a local restaurant. During our meal, the entire conversation focused on the safe deposit box. Lucille and I went back and forth, inside and out, up and down, trying to figure out what had happened at the bank, and why. Lucille was unclear on any details. She didn't seem to understand the extent of the dastardly deed. How I wish she had. Instead, she kept bragging about how good the chicken dinner was.

At least the chicken dinner had provided her with a little enjoyment. It showed on her face. Now, inside the car, I turned to a possible solution again.

"What are you going to ask Drake when you get home?"

"Where did you put my money?"

"Okay, you got it."

Knowing that he would say something mean, I encouraged her to keep asking about her money. She repeated the question. At approximately five o'clock, I stopped in front of Lucille's home. It was the end of a beautiful late summer day, with some light still outside. Lucille maneuvered out of the car. I handed her the walker. She grabbed it and swayed toward the steps. I followed close behind to catch her if she fell, and used my key to enter the house.

When we got inside, it was as if Lucille had a mission and she was focused on carrying it out. She walked straight to Drake's hovel, where he was lying down watching television. I thought, Okay, Lucille, it's your turn to take center stage. You know what to do.

Without a word from me, Lucille asked Drake the question she had cemented in her brain.

"Where'd you put my money?"

"I put it up?" Drake snapped back.

She wasn't satisfied with his answer. "Where did you put my money?"

From the way he answered, it was obvious he was playing her. I was filled with frustration and aggravation. He played along, knowing he was now in control of her life savings.

"I put it where you told me to put it."

"I didn't tell you to touch my money. Where'd you put it?"

He became visibly agitated. His voice rose, and his lip quivered. He sprang up, leaving the room where he was being interrogated. He started out the door, but paused. I guess he realized he had nowhere to go.

I tried to make Lucille comfortable by putting her to bed on propped-up pillows. I had to live with the fact that Lucille's life savings were gone, and Drake wasn't going to tell her what he did with the $70,000. And to make matters worse, Lucille was depending on me to get the money back. During the eight years since I had started taking care of her affairs, I had never touched a dime. I truly didn't think he would go that far either.

The very thought of having another reason to deal with Drake was enough to make me want to check out of this world. It was overwhelming. What could I do?

Chapter 19

I never dreamed that I would be here at the local police department doing what I was about to do. I filed a police report alleging grand larceny against Drake. That was no dream, nor did my actions have the stamp of approval from my family. In fact, filing a police report on a family member was going to have lasting repercussions. Well, right is right. Justice is justice. I was going to do it!

My husband went with me, for two reasons: First, for moral support, and second, to ensure that I didn't break down when I told the officers why I was visiting. Lately, I found myself bursting into tears over far less serious matters.

The 77th Precinct in Watts was a fairly new police station. As I left the car, I gazed at the building. It was a building for criminals. If there were no crimes, I thought, police departments would go out of business. New police stations, just like this one, were being built to accommodate individuals caught on the wrong side of the law—and that included Drake Black, my older brother.

For that reason, I was sad to be there. Yes, I know I said that this was a *new* building, but not everything wears *new* well. When thoughts of *new* come into my mind – such as a new office building, a new house, or a new car -- I think of fresh, sleek, innovative, and exciting, but not with this building. It represented the first step of incarceration for criminals. In a new home, you think about the square footage, how big this room or that room is. With that *new* building, none of that mattered. It was a place built for the lawless—like my brother.

Today, my arthritic knees were in rare form. But the pain in my heart was worse. I was broken-hearted and distressed. I continued up the steps with my husband's assistance. I thought how nice it would be to spend this gorgeous afternoon cutting back my roses. But this kind of day had been happening to me a lot in the past few months, and I couldn't seem to get it straightened out. I was always busy coming to Lucille's aid. Yes, I was duty bound to report Drake's theft to the proper authorities.

As I passed the plate glass windows, I hesitated, knowing there was no turning back. Then I hobbled to the counter for check-in and filled in the list with my name, date, and time of visit. As I turned around, I spotted my husband. He had found two seats in the crowded hallway. That was great. It meant I could rest my aching knees until the clerk called my name. I murmured and sat down to get comfortable. But how do you get comfortable in a police station? I reminded myself that I had to try and relax because I was a visitor and not a resident.

Okay, so why was I feeling so nervous and awkward? I needed to center my thoughts and keep my focus. I called on Jesus in my mind. "Jesus."

As we sat and waited, police officers were constantly coming from one place in the building and leaving for another. Though the police department wasn't somewhere I envisioned myself being, I was, nonetheless, going to stay there and see the job through.

From where I was seated, I could see the counter where I had checked in. There was nothing unique about the counter. Truthfully, it was rather forgettable. But I needed to retain that memory. It wasn't at all what I wanted, but it was what I had come here to do.

I couldn't rid myself of the thoughts of what had brought me to this place. My mind was a landscape that would forever bear the imprint of what would happen today. My memories were prominently parked in the front of my brain. I never wanted to be the subject of this symbolic artwork. This is not what I had envisioned. Today, I have to stay here long enough to make Drake pay the money back.

The officer called my name–Danielle Carrington. I passed the counter going toward him. Although the cold metal counter separated me from the officer, I felt a strange warmth come over me. I thought to myself, this officer will hear my story and confirm that I have done the right thing.

"Ma'am, what can I do for you?"

In my own words, I told the officer about Lucille's money being stolen. I told him that what he could do for me was to file charges against Drake and take this case to the District Attorney's office for criminal prosecution. But, then, I reminded myself to slow down because I was getting ahead of myself. And, so, I explained the nature of my concern. The officer listened. Was he listening because my complaints were rooted in something that required a closer look, or out of courtesy?

Finally, the officer directed me upstairs to the detective bureau. Even though I heard the officer direct me upstairs, I wondered just how I was going to get up those stairs. But I had to get up there because that's where justice sat. I wanted justice for Lucille. I took the first step for justice, one step at a time upstairs–aching body parts and all.

My husband and I walked cautiously through a door marked *Detective Bureau,* and I handed a female detective the intake sheet. I spilled out the Drake-Lucille story, and she followed with a trail of questions.

"You think he stole the money? Where do they live? Where do you live?" She looked over the answers I had given. "How did he get the money?"

"He took the money and papers out of the safe deposit box, and closed out the box."

I made sure to tell the detective that Lucille was an 87-year-old, feeble lady. After the detective completed the initial report, she told me that a formal report would be prepared, and a copy could be obtained later at police headquarters.

"Thank you," I said, and limped out. Surely, in the warmth of the late afternoon, the pre-mature arthritis would leave. What could be worse than premature menopause than premature arthritis? Well in a little while, I would be able to walk without pain.

Chapter 20

September 27, 2004: Dear God, I'm in the depths of it, and I feel like I am sinking. Where are you? Danielle kept writing.

I received a call from the detectives at the 77th Precinct Detective Bureau. They asked me to meet them at Lucille's house at 10:30 that morning. They planned to interview Lucille about the missing money from the safe deposit box. I rushed to shower, dress, and get to Lucille's house on time. I wanted her to know she was not alone. By 10:15, I had hit the streets.

By 10:35, I had reached Lucille's house. The police had already arrived and were conducting the interview with Lucille. She was in her living room, sitting in her favorite chair, and Drake was nowhere to be found. I walked towards Lucille and noticed that she looked disheveled, in a faded blue chenille robe. Her underclothes peeked from underneath. She looked like she had been in a fight, and her opponent had won. Her long, thinning grey hair was scattered over her head. Her house smelled rancid, like stale meat.

I stood in the hallway so she could see me, and she smiled faintly. Why had Drake left her in the room alone to speak with strangers? Or, had they asked him to leave?

Detective Morton took Lucille through a short mental acuity exam. "How old are you?"

Lucille searched the room, the walls, the floor, and her fingernails, as if the answer could be found in one of those places.

"Do you know who the president is?"

"Clinton." Right office, wrong person.

Detective Gonzo, standing beside me, asked, "Is there anyone else in the house?"

"Yes."

"Ask them to come out because we want to see everyone in the house."

I knocked on Drake's door. There was no answer. I knocked again.

"Y-e-s-s-s," he yelled.

"The police want you to come into the living room."

He finally came out, moving like molasses, surly, and made his way into the living room.

"Sit down, Mr. Black."

Drake looked out the window, still standing.

"Sit down, Mr. Black." Something must have clicked in Drake's brain that he was actually dealing with the police, who had guns. He sat, a snide look stretched over his face.

Detective Morton continued questioning Lucille. "What's your name?"

The shade over Lucille's mental state slightly lifted. "Lucille."

"Do you know how much money was in your safe deposit box?"

"Oh, about three or four hundred dollars." She saw me and asked, "Is that right, Danielle?"

"No, it was seventy thousand dollars."

The detective turned to Drake. "What did you do with her money?"

"It's put up."

"Put up where?" Detective Gonzo asked.

"I put it where she told me to put it."

It was embarrassing to watch Detective Gonzo's annoyance. She abruptly said they were leaving and asked me to step outside with them.

We walked outside and down the steps toward the chain-linked fence.

"We had to leave because if we had stayed, there would have been an altercation.

Somebody was going to get hurt and it wasn't going to be me," Detective Gonzo said. "Because you and Drake are sister and brother, we can't do anything."

"I don't understand that. It makes no sense to me," I argued.

Detective Gonzo ignored my argument. "You should immediately file for conservatorship."

"Thank you for coming," I said.

"Don't go back inside. I think she'll be safe with him long enough for you to make arrangements."

I had no intention of going inside, other than to get my personal belongings. But Drake made sure I didn't come back. He threw my purse and sweater on the porch and locked the door. I gathered them and headed home to plan my next move.

Chapter 21

Drake's last saga with the police shook me to the core. I had had enough of him. I thought it was quite okay to give myself some time to recuperate from those blinding headaches, waking up screaming at three o'clock in the morning without being able to get back to sleep, weight gain, increased appetite, nightmares. To me, I seemed worse than a kid screaming because she thought she saw a monster. The night screams frightened my family. They didn't know what was happening to me, and neither did I.

When I finally got to sleep, it wasn't restful. How could I sleep restfully when I had the weight of Lucille's world on my shoulders? Her situation was using me like a wound-up toy. I told myself things were improving, but I knew better. It was ugly. If this tragedy was shaking my world, I could only imagine what it was doing to Lucille's. Unfortunately, she couldn't express her feelings, and I couldn't get rid of mine. But through the sight of the impossible, I determined to fight to the end.

I dug deep within myself because I felt that who I really was called on me to step forward, like no other time. Would I be able to diminish the tragedy of this helpless woman and make a difference? Lucille must be the face of millions like her, I thought. Would my fight help others who take care of their loved ones? Would it warn them of the danger signs ahead? Could my efforts help to bring safety and dignity into their lives? I felt like a loner in my fight against the wicked, but somehow, I knew there were other old people out there. I had to rebound. Although this tragedy was thrust on me without warning or permission, I had to triumph over it.

I reminded myself, "Girlfriend, being tortured by this is not at all who you are." But hearing that didn't spring me into action. I still felt lifeless. I felt as if I were being tossed in a storm, and weather predictions were not good. My fair weather friends wondered what I did to cause such problems in my life. That didn't bother me. The issue was about Lucille. Was I going to get strong enough to make a difference? Well, that's what survivors do, I told myself. They find a way to come back through God's witty inventions, His power, and His strength.

Each day that followed had its own set of agendas and priorities. But I felt like I was in a daze. I wanted to stay in bed. I was tired and broken. Then another curve ball hit me square in the face.

* * *

October 1, 2004: The Los Angeles County Sheriff's Deputy from the Civil Processing Unit came to my home, my sanctuary, to serve me with an *Order to Show Cause (Civil Harassment) and Request for a Temporary Restraining Order.*

When the doorbell rang, I answered it.

"Are you Danielle Carrington?"

"Yes." I focused on the officer, but my insides were screaming. No, he didn't! No, he didn't! I was furious. The officer served the papers and left. In my hands was the document Drake had filed. I knew it was him. *Request for a Temporary Restraining Order*. I was being ordered to appear in court on October 19, 2004, at 8:30 a.m. in Department 6, Room 247, in the Superior Court located at 111 North Hill Street, Los Angeles, CA.

I have never had so much as a scrape with the law and, now, I have been ordered to court. The further I read, the more I realized that the document was riddled with bogus charges, filed by Drake under the guise of Lucille's name. He was defaming her name, against her wishes. Until it was settled in court, I was given orders not to do any of the following:

"Harass, molest, attack, strike, threaten, sexually assault, batter, follow, stalk, destroy the personal property of, disturb the peace of, keep under surveillance, or block movements in public places or thoroughfares."

Further, I was not to:

"Contact, telephone, or communicate by any means (including mail, fax, or e-mail) except for peaceful written contact through a process server or other person for legal papers related to a court case."

I read further and discovered that Lucille didn't want me at her house anymore. Well, who would take care of her? Judge Jane on the *People's Court* characterized Drake best when she said, "I wouldn't believe you if your tongue were notarized."

Now, by Drake's keeping me away, Lucille was relegated solely into his hands. I worried for her safety. I didn't know what he had in mind, or how far he might go, or what he would actually do to her.

I knew there was no way on God's green earth that Lucille had anything to do with that document. It was nobody but Drake.

Just a few lines down, Drake listed himself as the person who needed to be protected from me. That strapping 6'2", 270-pound man needed protecting from me? I am only 5'4" in heels, so that had to be insane. Nothing could ever justify such allegations.

Now Lucille was supposed to be articulating her thoughts. She could never do that, as she couldn't even say how much money was in her safe deposit box. Now, though, she could file a document that said with great clarity that I was harassing her. She was lucid enough to request that I be brought before a judge to answer for "untoward behavior."

"...Causing her undue harassment, emotional distress, and elder adult abuse."

The document alleged that I came to Lucille's residence on September 27, 2004, asking for the plaintiff to turn over her money and the deed to her home to me. It also stated that I am Lucille's niece and the Administrator of her living trust that Lucille wants removed from that document.

Was that the living trust Lucille called me about after I returned from vacation on July 9, 2004? How did it get twisted that I wanted the deed to her house, as well as her money turned over to me?

Would that be the money in the safe deposit box that Drake emptied on September 20, 2004? That money and the deed to her house, along with other personal papers, had been in Lucille's safe deposit box for years, and was now in Drake's possession But I was the one with the key to the box and could have taken anything I wanted, whenever I wanted. I never did.

The document alleged that I was guilty of wanting all of Lucille's personal belongings, but it was just the opposite. I had taken care of those things for eight years, and now Drake wanted to block me from stopping him from taking them all. He had already emptied her safe deposit box. He had taken it all. His allegations were as preposterous as his actions. He wants something that I don't know about, I thought. What is it?

The document also alleged that I was *"threatening Lucille about removing herself from her home and placing her at a convalescent home, and all of this against her will."* Whoever wrote that needed a serious course in English grammar. The misspelled words and the grammatical errors were atrocious. If Lucille had actually authored the document, I could have excused her because she is an 87-year-old Depression-era survivor. But anyone else—

The document also alleged that the "plaintiff *Lucille will suffer great and irreparable harm before this petition can be heard in court, unless the court makes the temporary orders requested below and those orders are:*

"If Defendant isn't ordered to stop harassing me immediately, I will suffer a nervous breakdown. I'm afraid when they come over to my house, because they mean no good for my well-being. I'm an 87-year-old widow that wants to live my last days in peace."

Well, Lucille, my dear, I am not the one you need to be concerned about. I mean nothing but good for you. Your enemy is living right in your house. And if you could, I know you would watch out for him.

According to the court, I had more restrictions: "S*tay at least 50 yards away from the following persons and places: 8510 Menlo Avenue, Los Angeles, California.*

Drake must have meant to seal Lucille's fate with that document, dated September 29, 2004, two days after the police detectives visited him in her home to question him about the missing money from her safe deposit box. Well, they didn't have to worry about me violating the court's Temporary Restraining Order. I proudly declared that I live within the boundaries of the law. I still worried about Lucille, though, especially now.

Chapter 22

During the days before the court hearing for the restraining order, I was busy gathering information, but not knowing what to expect. My head felt like it was going to explode. It pounded like a jackhammer hitting a block of cement. The tangled thoughts in my head were exhausting. They beat out a constant phrase: "You want my money, you want my money, you want my money. Stay away. Stay away."

My heart wanted to play out the words of the restraining order, as if Lucille actually wrote the document, and my mind played into it. I had been the one involved in Lucille's life, taking care of her business affairs since her husband passed in 1996, eight years before. I felt like all of my efforts had gone unappreciated. I had spent countless days at her home when her main sewer line broke, and I had to search for a plumber, interview the company, and negotiate prices on her behalf. And what about taking her to Sears to buy a washer and dryer? I was even there when they made the delivery and discovered that she had a busted gas line. I took care of it.

"Danielle, I just don't know what I'd do without you!" Now I believed such words were just trite clichés used to placate me. But that's okay, Lucille. I did that and a myriad of other things for you because you deserved to have somebody reliable in your life. And what about taking her to have her living trust created?

No, no. I shouldn't take this out on Lucille. She trusted me explicitly. I never gave her cause not to.

And what about taking her to all those doctor and dental appointments, and specialized medical appointments, and picking up her prescriptions? Had she forgotten all of that? Or, had she decided to fold up her mind and forget that I ever did anything to bring her peace and safety?

"Danielle, you just too good to me. I don't know what I'd do without you."

I obliged her, assured her, and helped her. I was constantly shuffling my calendar dates to accommodate her. I was duty bound to aid and assist her, each and every time she needed me. I pushed back my tears.

I managed to crack a smile, though, recalling one of the many times I received a phone call from her.

"Danielle, I got some old letter in the mail and I don't know what it is. When can you come by and look at it?"

I had become a pretty good time juggler, a multi-tasker. But anyone who multi-tasks knows that some days are better than others. Often, Lucille wanted me to drop everything and hurry over, but it wasn't always possible. I was working, cooking, driving children, and taking care of my household, and then I had pressing personal things to do.

"I'll try and come tomorrow." Sometimes my putting her off was sufficient, but at other times, she insisted on a definite, almost immediate time. When I made a promise to Lucille, I kept it.

"Danielle, you got to come over here and look and see what's wrong with this washing machine?" she told me one day.

Lucille had another plumbing problem. I discovered that the $7,000 plumbing job she had had done in 1997 had come back to haunt her with a vengeance. The pipe in her bathroom was leaking. She had already replaced her main sewage line. So why was this plumbing problem reappearing?

Nat had used Do Right Plumbing Company when he was alive, and after his death, Lucille called them for her every plumbing need. They had charged $7,000 to replace her main sewer line. I didn't find out about it until after the fact.

When I called Do Right Plumbing, they claimed ignorance about my complaint. I reminded them of the $7,000 they had charged back in 1997 for the main sewer line. They wouldn't hear of fixing the problem for free. They played hardball. It took me months of grief to make them do the right thing. To me, it was just another problem that I had become used to solving for Lucille.

Now she was seeing my visits to her house as harassment? The very nature of the word *harassment* was rooted in someone's deliberate intention to cause danger or to bring harm to a person. It was all I could do to keep myself from hating Lucille.

But then I thought, how absolutely foolish of me to entertain such devious thoughts about Lucille. I knew, deep in my heart, that she had nothing to do with preparing or sending that restraining order. She had never said one unkind word to me, not even when I was a child. She never said, "Danielle, I don't want you to do nothing else for me," or "Danielle, don't come back to my house."

Yes, she did appreciate me. Yes, she did love me, and I loved her. She was the aunt who opened up the world to me as a child.

She had the strength I wanted to have when I grew up. Now was the time to prove it.

I realized I was foolish for blaming Lucille, as Drake would do anything to keep me away from her until he cleaned her out of all her worldly wealth. Well, I had to find the Lucille-kind-of strength to meet him at the point of his greed.

Chapter 23

What Drake and his girlfriend/ex-wife had done to Lucille couldn't be ignored. They couldn't get away with abusing her financially and mentally. I had no choice but to do what I had done—having the theft from her safe deposit box investigated. I didn't initiate a legal problem for Drake, as some of the family members seemed to think. Drake initiated one. I reacted to block him from abusing Lucille.

I called my attorney and instructed him to file an Elder Abuse lawsuit against Drake and his partner, alleging theft of all of Lucille's money from her safe deposit box. I knew that act would begin another round of head banging with Drake. But it had to be done. I was still reeling from being summoned to court as the DEFENDANT in a Restraining Order hearing for harassing Lucille. Every time I thought about that document, I felt crushed all over again. I felt like I was sitting in the middle of an inferno, with no escape.

After asking me a lot of questions, my attorney decided I had a case. Where would all of this end up? How much more aggravation and frustration could I endure? How much more money would I have to spend? The attorneys weren't cheap.

Besides filing my own lawsuit, I had to answer Lucille's allegations in the phony Request for a Temporary Restraining Order. I began to gather my character references. Number one was

Isabelle. She was Lucille's niece who had kept close to Lucille and me. Although I knew the allegations in the Restraining Order were false, they stung, nonetheless. They were beyond any realm of reasonableness. I wondered whether Drake ever told Lucille what he was saying and doing. Did he demand that she sign the document without telling her what it was? I know he just signed the document, not giving Lucille the respect of her opinion.

* * *

October 19, 2004: Dear God, I thought you would have answered my prayers by now, but here we are with a legal battle stretched out several years into the future. I wish you would intervene and give us justice. Allow Lucille to know a bit of joy before she leaves this world. Please. Your servant, Danielle... She wrote until midnight, and before realizing it, she drifted off to sleep.

Now that the court date had arrived, I was fine. My attorney and husband were both there. That morning, we tried to find reasonably priced parking in the downtown area, but it was almost impossible. I decided that the cost for parking couldn't become an issue. We just needed to get into the courthouse and meet with my attorney.

"There's parking in there," I said to my husband, pointing to the busy parking structure near the courthouse. We parked, got out of the car, and rushed into the courthouse.

A long line of people were trying to do exactly what we were doing, entering the Grand Halls of Marble. We took our place in line. I tried to peer over the tall men standing in front of us to see whether there was a second line or a shorter one, but there wasn't. To my left, the line was moving, so we stepped into it. Facing us must have been 100 steps to climb. I worried that my knees would lock up, and I would fall down, but I had zero choice.

After a slow climb, we made it to the landing. My knees were in pain and my back was hurting, but I had made it to answer the summons. The long walk down the corridor of justice provided warmth in a cold sort of way. The walls spoke of justice. Today, I was looking for justice, where the innocent would be set free and the guilty locked away. I entered the hallways as the "guilty." Would I be as optimistic when I came out, or would Drake's lies be so convincing that the judge would bow in submission?

As we approached the courtroom, a cold block of cement invited us to sit down and rest our weary bodies. I didn't sit, but looked around and thought, where is Lucille? Surely, the person making these outlandish allegations will be here?

The hallway was filled with tons of people waiting to enter the courts of justice. I still didn't see Lucille. Well, I was there. That's all I was responsible for. And what about Isabelle, Lucille's niece? I didn't see her either. Isabelle and her daughter Marjorie were Lucille's relatives, and they lived a couple of blocks from her. They were supposed to be there to vouch for my character, and I was anxious for them to appear.

Just as I finished my thoughts, the courtroom bailiff opened the double doors to Judge Silverman's courtroom. We grabbed seats near the front row center and the crowd took all the others.

As I looked around the courtroom, I still didn't see Isabelle or her daughter Marjorie.

Inside the courtroom, I reminded myself to strap in, relax, and get ready for the ride of my life. Then I spotted Isabelle and Marjorie. The bailiff called the courtroom to order. Judge Silverman was an older man, still spry, and wearing bifocals. He took his seat on the bench. After the seventh case, the court clerk called the case of *Lucille Stanton vs. Danielle Carrington*. It was so strange hearing that. It was unbelievable.

"Will the parties take their places at the counselor's table?"

I got up and moved to the end of the table where my attorney was sitting, where the DEFENDANT sits. I didn't take offense at the title because it wasn't who I was. Oh, that wasn't true. I did take offense. Just then, Drake rolled Lucille in a wheelchair to the counselor's table. My eyes locked with Lucille's. I checked Lucille's clothes to see if she looked neat. She didn't. And my insides wept. She seemed to be asking, "Where am I? What am I doing here?"

After Drake parked Lucille at the counselor's table, he sat in one of the remaining chairs.

My attorney sprang to his feet. "Your Honor, Mr. Black is going to be called as a witness. I will be cross-examining him, so he needs to be dismissed."

"All right. Mr. Black, because you're going to be a witness in this matter, I have to ask you to step outside," the judge said.

Drake's face said he didn't appreciate that call one bit. Isabelle, also a witness, made her way outside. The questioning had begun, and Drake was still sitting there.

"Ms. Stanton, is there anyone you would like me to speak to today?" Judge Silverman asked.

"What?" Lucille asked.

"Is there anyone you would like to have me speak to today?"

"To speak for me?" Lucille asked.

"To speak for you, or to give me testimony as to what's happened. Is there anybody here?"

"She's turning to my client," Attorney Barnes said.

That moment reminded me of the time when the police detectives came to Lucille's house after the safe deposit box theft and asked her a question she couldn't answer. She looked for me.

"Excuse me, judge," Drake blurted out.

"Danielle Carrington," Lucille said.

"Ms. Stanton wants Danielle Carrington to speak," Attorney Barnes said.

"Can we have a continuance so I can get my aunt proper legal representation, please?" Drake asked.

"No. Not right now. I'm going to have to talk to Ms. Stanton. I'll see. Believe me, Mr. Black, I'm going to be fair to her. Now please step outside—Mr. Barnes, are you aware of any conservatorship proceedings currently going on?"

"There are none. But, your honor, we do have two documents attached as exhibits. One is a Power of Attorney, which has been duly executed and notarized by Ms. Stanton, appointing Danielle Carrington to be in charge of the person and property of Ms. Stanton." He paused.

"Secondly, your honor, I've attached a living trust. And calling your honor's attention to the provisions of that living trust, specifically, if I may, on page eight, article five, section 501. The trustee, who is the defendant in this matter, shall upon the death, resignation, or incapacity of the trustor, have the right to perform the duties of trustee. The trustor hereby appoints as successor trustee, my client, Danielle Carrington. Your honor, we attached a rather extensive declaration to our response indicating that since 1996—"

"I read the declaration," the judge interrupted.

"In addition, we attached a copy of a police report dealing with what has occurred," Attorney Barnes said.

"I'm continuing with the hearing. But I'm coming off the bench to talk to Ms. Stanton," the judge said. He walked down and stood in front of Lucille.

"Do you know who I am? What I do here?"

"Yes," Lucille said, smiling. "You the judge."

"That's right. Okay. And who brought you here this morning?"

"My nephew."

"Your nephew."

"Uh-huh."

"What is his name?"

"Drake Black."

"Okay. Do you know why he brought you to see me?"

"Yeah?" Lucille answered with uncertainty.

"Tell me why."

"To get my will and everything straightened out."

"To get your will and everything straightened out?"

"I think that's what it is," Lucille nodded.

"But you're not too sure why you're here, right?"

"What?" Lucille asked.

"You're not exactly sure why your nephew brought you to see me today?" the judge repeated.

"Well, he don't want nobody to take my property or nothing like that."

"And are you afraid somebody is going to take your property?"

"Well, I don't know. You know, when you get up in age."

"I don't think you're that old."

"You know, they try to take everything you got."

"Uh-huh," the judge agreed.

"So I have to have somebody to try to protect it."

"Okay. All right."

"And that's my nephew, Drake Black."

"Is there anybody else that's been helping you over the years?"

"Drake Black takes care of me. He lives with me."

"Is there anybody else? What about Danielle Carrington?"

"She don't live with me."

"Does she help take care of you?"

Lucille shook her head negatively.

"Did she ever–in the past–take care of you?"

"Well, I had a husband. And then, after my husband passed, then my nephew took over."

"How many years were you married?"

"I married in 1949."

"When did your husband pass?"

"My husband passed—he's been dead about twenty years."

Lucille didn't know this was October 2004, that her husband died in 1996, and that Drake didn't come to help her until 2004. She couldn't put it all together in sequence.

"Okay, so you were married about 35, 40 years?"

"Yes."

"Good for you. How many children did you have?"

"Not any."

"None. How many nieces and nephews do you have?"

"Oh, Lord. A lot!"

"That's good. You sit tight. I'm going back up to my seat." The judge sat in his chair, lifted his sleeve, and checked his watch. Then he got right into where he left off. I was feeling a bit better, stronger.

"All right. Mrs. Carrington, under your Power of Attorney, have you attempted to get medical assistance for your aunt?" Judge Silverman asked.

I sat up straight and cleared my voice and mind. "I've taken her to the doctor since her husband died back in 1996. Up until the time Mr. Black moved in with her, I was the one."

"Right. But in June, she was examined. And I have progress reports. And clearly they raise questions as to whether her mental capacity is appropriate for the person."

"Right," Attorney Barnes said.

"There is no testimony from the doctors anywhere in her progress reports as to incapacity. I find that she's confused as to why she's here. But she seems otherwise to know who she is and know who I am. She's just a little confused as to what today's hearing is about."

"Your Honor, there is the recommendation from the convalescent hospital doctor that the patient is not safe to live by herself," Attorney Barnes said.

"It says she shouldn't live by herself," Judge Silverman said.

"Correct," Mr. Barnes added.

"That is not a determination of mental capacity," Judge Silverman said.

"I understand," Mr. Barnes agreed.

"I want to know why she was examined for that purpose, Ms. Carrington."

"You'd have to ask –" I started.

"In regard to the financial affairs, Ms. Carrington has continued to pay all of the bills. Took care of all the financial responsibilities. Paid all of the utilities. Done everything for Ms. Stanton. She was the only one with legal access to that safe deposit box, except Ms. Stanton," Attorney Barnes said. "That was done with Ms. Stanton's consent in 1996, when her husband passed. Her signature notarized on the Power of Attorney was just to create additional proof."

"I guess that's what I don't understand," the judge said. "I mean, Ms. Carrington, your claims are that Mr. Black is taking advantage of Ms. Stanton."

"Yes."

"But you have Power of Attorney to control Ms. Stanton's personal relationships and
affairs."

"Yes, absolutely."

"You seem to have all the power you need to eliminate Mr. Black's presence and take care of Ms. Stanton in an appropriate manner as of right now," Judge Silverman said. "So I don't quite understand why you haven't done that."

Attorney Barnes answered. "Those arrangements were made shortly after the last visit, where Ms. Stanton was to come and live with Ms. Carrington and her family. Then this document was filed. And at that point, I instructed Ms. Carrington not to take any steps until today's hearing."

"I see. So, in other words, if you're not so restricted, Ms. Carrington, you're prepared today right after this hearing to take control and custody of Ms. Stanton?" the judge asked.

"Absolutely."

An overwhelming power floated around in the air, coming from the judge, regardless of what Lucille had said, regardless of what anyone thought. I felt righteousness in the air, some miraculous favor in the atmosphere.

Judge Silverman shifted his attention to Lucille. He looked at his watch and lowered his sleeve again. My body shook, as I didn't know what was about to happen. I did know, though, that something major was on tap.

Attorney Barnes began to question Lucille. "Ms. Stanton, I'm going to ask you a few questions. First of all, do you know who that woman is?"

"That's my niece."

"Do you know how long you've known her?"

"Ever since she was a baby."

"Okay. Now, your husband passed a little while ago. I'm sorry to have heard about that."

"Yeah."

"Since then, had Ms. Carrington—Did she ever take you to the doctors?—Did she drive you to the doctors?"

"Yes."

"Okay, did she ever take you shopping?"

"Yes."

"Did you ask her to pay your bills?"

"No."

"No. Did she ever pay any of the bills for you?"

"I don't know. Did you?" Lucille looked to me for confirmation.

"I did."

"Do you remember doing what's called a living trust? That was a document you might have gone to a lawyer for."

"A living trust?" she asked.

"Yes."

"Do I have one?"

"That's a good question. Do you know if you have a living trust?"

"I think so. Don't I have one?" She looked at me.

I nodded.

"When you did, did you want Ms. Carrington to take care of things, so in case something happened to you, she would be in charge?"

"Well, I tell you what. I got my nephew staying there with me."

"Yeah."

"And I really haven't made up my mind what I want to do."

"You haven't made up your mind?" Attorney Barnes asked.

"No."

"I'm going to show you something. See if you can recognize your signature, okay?"

"Okay."

"Will that be all right?"

"Let me get my glasses."

"You want to borrow mine?" Attorney Barnes asked.

"I don't want to borrow yours."

Judge Silverman intervened. "Let's go quickly through this part, Mr. Barnes. I have examined Ms. Stanton. I think I have a good sense of her capacity."

"Yes," Attorney Barnes said. "Okay. Turn to the last page here. Is that your signature?"

"That's mine," Lucille said.

"Okay. Very good. One other thing I want to show you is this." He handed her a document. "Do you remember going with Ms. Carrington to sign this document that's called a power of attorney?" Attorney Barnes asked.

"Evidently. My name's there."

The judge asked, "Ms. Stanton, do you understand what that document says? That document we were just talking about says that Danielle Carrington is going to be the one to help you handle all your papers."

"Can you say that—"

"That document says by law that you want Danielle Carrington to take care and help you with writing checks on your properties and things like that," Attorney Barnes said.

"Well, I got my nephew staying with me now."

"Right," Attorney Barnes said.

"So, I don't think I need her right now," Lucille said.

"Ms. Stanton, do you trust Danielle, your niece?"

"Oh, yeah. I trust her."

"Thank you, Ms. Stanton. Your Honor, I have nothing more."

When Judge Silverman called a recess, I was so tired I couldn't react, but just walked out in the hall and went to the bathroom. I splashed water on my face and shook my legs and hands. I ached everywhere, in every bone in my body. I took two Tylenols.

Chapter 24

We returned to the courtroom in fifteen minutes. Without much fanfare, the session was called to order.

"The court calls Danielle Carrington to the witness stand."

The air was mixed with an odd combination of confusion and clarity. Hopefully, clarity would win. I walked towards the witness stand, which was located on the opposite end of the courtroom. The walk seemed longer than it actually was.

"Would you raise your right hand," the bailiff asked.

"Do you swear to tell the truth, the whole truth, and nothing but the truth, so help you God?"

"I do."

I thought to myself, I sure do affirm to tell nothing but the pure, unadulterated truth. It's the only way to live life. I couldn't wait to answer. I couldn't wait for the truth to be revealed.

Attorney Barnes began his questioning. "Ms. Carrington, are you related to the plaintiff, Lucille Stanton?"

"I am."

"In what way?"

"She is my aunt."

"Is this your mother's sister?"

"This is my dad's older sister."

"All right. And your uncle passed; is that correct?"

"Yes."

"When did he pass?"

"I believe it was October 15th of 1996."

"All right. Since 1996, Ms. Carrington, have you assisted the plaintiff in her financial affairs?"

"I have."

"In what ways?"

"I've basically handled everything for her. Taking her to the doctor. Making sure she had medications. Ensuring that her bills were paid. Making sure when the furnace went out to call the gas company. Things like that."

"Is there a mortgage on the house?"

"There is no mortgage."

"So, whatever household bills, who would pay those since her husband died?" Attorney Barnes asked.

"Initially, she was able to do it. I would write the checks out as far as *Pay to the Order of*. She would sign them.

"Then what happened?"

"Like I said, after the bathtub incident, I began writing them out totally."

"Do you have a joint bank account with the plaintiff?"

"No."

"Did you write those checks on her bank account?"

"Yes."

"And would you assure those would be sent out?"

"I would ensure that, yes."

"You're familiar with the exhibit that is a living trust; is that correct?"

"I am."

"Okay. Did you go with Lucille Stanton to have her sign that living trust?"

"I took her. Yes."

"All right. And that was her wish for you to be the successor trustee?"

"It was her wish. Yes, definitely her wish."

"Did you hold any undue influence over her when she signed that?"

"Absolutely not."

"She did that free and clear?"

"Absolutely."

"All right. There also is a Power of Attorney. Did she ask you to have that prepared?"

"I basically shared with her that it was time that we needed to do something to ensure that she was taken care of."

"All right."

"And she agreed."

"Did she understand that?" Attorney Barnes asked.

"She understood."

"Did someone read or explain to her what that power of attorney was?"

"I did."

"Okay. And was her signature notarized?"

"Yes."

"All right. Did she, at that point, understand what was going on?" Attorney Barnes

asked.

"I explained the whole process."

"Okay. Did you do that in front of anybody?"

"In front of the notary."

"And at the time the Power of Attorney was executed, she had a bank account; is that correct?"

"She had two bank accounts."

"Did you have access to those bank accounts?"

"I had access to the bank accounts, yes."

"And you used that solely for her care?"

"Solely for her care."

"Did you ever make any withdrawals at any time from 1996 to the present on your own behalf and not for the plaintiff?"

"Absolutely not."

"You also were aware there was a safe deposit box. Is that correct?

"Yes."

"Who had access to that box?" Mr. Barnes asked.

"The safe deposit box could be accessed by Lucille Stanton and myself."

"Did you ever take anything out of that safe deposit box?"

"I think it was two weeks before late September, I went to the box to ensure that everything was intact, because the key was missing."

"What were the contents of that safe deposit box that you checked?"

"A pink slip that she was giving a car to one of my sister's sons. There was a death certificate and a marriage certificate. And also there was seventy thousand dollars in cash."

"What was the source of that money, do you know?"

"I don't know for sure. But I know that her husband did this when he was alive to ensure she was taken care of."

"Did you ever take any part of that money out?"

"Absolutely not."

"She had sufficient funds in her bank account?" Mr. Barnes asked.

"Yes, she did."

"Did you ever have to assist her financially in any way?"

"No."

"Did you have any discussions with your husband about having Ms. Stanton come live with you?"

"I did."

"When was that decided?"

"This was decided, approximately, just maybe a week before I was served with the restraining order."

"Did you have an opportunity to communicate that to Ms. Stanton?"

"I did not."

"And this was okay with your family and your husband to have her come live with you; is that correct?"

"Yes."

"Now, the last time you were in the safe deposit box – by the way, whose key was missing, your key or someone else's?"

"It was Ms. Stanton's key."

"So you actually went with Ms. Stanton?"

"I took Ms. Stanton with me."

"To the bank?"

"Yes."

"To get another box?"

"Exactly."

"And what happened?"

"I was told that she came in the day before with Mr. Black, who had emptied the box."

"And were any contents left in the box at all?"

"The entire account was closed, and another box was not opened."

"What did you do, if anything?"

"I shared the information with Ms. Stanton."

"What did she say?"

"She cried and said she couldn't believe Drake had done that, and could I get her money back."

"In the past 3 months, did Ms. Stanton ever tell you or give you any complaints about Mr. Black living with her?"

"Yes."

"What were those complaints?"

"She would often tell me, 'Danielle, you just don't know what I'm going through.'"

"And I would tell her, 'Aunt Lucille, I don't know unless you tell me what's going on.'"

"Up until finding out about the safe deposit box being closed, did you believe everything was at least going somewhat all right at the house with Mr. Black?"

"I had some reservations."

"What were those reservations?"

"In addition to the comments that she would make, when I would take her to the hair dresser and we would have that ride, she would share things with me. And she also said she was afraid of him."

"In what way?"

"Because there was an incident where she had gone into the kitchen to wash dishes. And Drake yelled, 'What in the hell are you doing? Get out of here right now.'"

"And do you remember when that occurred?"

"I don't remember the exact date, but it was some time during the month of August."

"Is it your desire under the powers granted to you under the Power of Attorney, assuming that there are no orders relating to this hearing today, to arrange for Ms. Stanton to come live with you?"

"Yes."

"Are you prepared to take her from this courtroom today?" Judge Silverman asked.

"Yes."

"You may be excused." I walked back and sat down.

Chapter 25

Judge Silverman stood and looked at a paper on the table in front of him. Then he walked out of the courtroom. The bailiff took care of the formalities, and everyone looked around. The judge returned without an explanation, and looked straight at Isabelle Montague.

"The court calls Isabelle Montague to the stand."

"Did you take an oath?" Mr. Barnes asked.

"Yes."

"Are you related to Lucille Stanton?"

"Yes."

"How are you related?"

"She's my aunt."

"Are you also related to Danielle Carrington?"

"Yes."

"How are you so related?"

"She's my cousin."

"Would you consider yourself friendly with Ms. Stanton?"

"Yes."

"And how often would you talk to Ms. Stanton, let's say, in the past year?"

"Every day up until she had to go to the hospital because she had an injury."

"So about June of 2004?"

She nodded. "After she came back, I would talk with her on the phone. Sometimes the phone was busy. And sometimes she didn't answer it."

"Do you know when in June of 2004?"

"Yes, June 25."

"Is that the time Mr. Black came to live with Ms. Stanton?"

"Yes."

"And is that when it became more difficult for you to contact Ms. Stanton?"

"Yes."

"Taking you back to the time after the unfortunate death of Ms. Stanton's husband, and up until June of 2004, were you aware of whether or not Mrs. Carrington was involved in any of the financial or personal activities of Ms. Stanton?"

"Yes."

"And how were you so aware?"

"I was aware because my Aunt Lucille Stanton would tell me, 'Well, Danielle is going to take me to the doctor, take me to the bank today, and then we're going to have lunch.' She always enjoyed that."

"During any of those phone conversations, did your aunt ever express any complaints about what Mrs. Carrington was doing for her?"

"No. She only said, 'I'm glad Danielle is here to take care of me.'"

"Okay. And were you aware that Danielle, in fact, was taking care of her financial problems or issues?"

"Yes."

"And how were you aware of that?"

"Because my aunt told me."

"As a family member, did you have any objection to Mrs. Carrington taking care of your aunt's finances?"

"No, I was happy."

"Did you feel Mrs. Carrington was trustworthy?"

"Yes, trustworthy and reliable. Very honest."

"Okay."

"Law-abiding citizen."

"Is there anything else you want to tell me, Ms. Montague? Anything you think is important to this case?" the judge asked.

"I think Mrs. Carrington should still be in charge of my aunt's affairs because my aunt does need someone who is honest and reliable and dependable, because I can't drive. And my cousin, she was very good about taking her to different places…"

"Do you think Ms. Stanton would enjoy living with Mrs. Carrington?" Judge Silverman asked.

"Yes."

"Ms. Montague, thank you so much for coming in. You are excused."

"Thank you."

* * *

In the following thirty minutes, the next witness was called. "The court calls to the witness stand, Drake Black."

The bailiff walked out into the hall to get him. Drake strolled in and took the witness stand.

"Mr. Black, were you here this morning to take the oath?"

"No, sir."

"Sir, if you'll raise your right hand," the clerk said.

Drake Black was sworn in and took a seat on the witness stand.

"Are you related to Lucille Stanton?"

"Yes."

"And how are you related?"

"She is my niece. I mean my nephew. I'm sorry, I'm her nephew. She's my aunt."

"When did you come to live with Ms. Stanton?"

"June of 2004?"

"There was an incident involving Ms. Stanton, where she fell in the bathtub. Are you aware of that?"

"Yes."

"Prior to coming to live with your aunt, where were you living?"

"Twenty-four-zero-one Watley Avenue, Coral Springs, California."

"Who lives there?"

"I did."

"Anybody else?"

"My mother and—."

"Are you currently employed?"

"No."

"When was the last time you were fully gainfully employed?"

"June of 2002."

"What were you employed as?"

"Bus operator."

"And is it true you've been on disability since 2002?"

"Yes."

"And who asked you to come to live with your aunt?"

"My auntie."

"Prior to coming to live with her, did you talk to your sister?"

"Yes, we talked."

"Now, were you aware, before you came to live with Ms. Stanton, that Mrs. Carrington was the trustee, the successor trustee under the living trust for Ms. Stanton?"

"No."

"Were you aware that at some time a power of attorney was executed by Ms. Stanton, appointing Mrs. Carrington her power of attorney?"

"No."

"Are you aware that those things exist now, Mr. Black?" Judge Silverman asked.

"Yes."

"How did you become aware of those things?"

"She expressed it."

"She?"

"Danielle Carrington expressed that information to me."

"When did she tell you that?"

"Few weeks ago."

"Was there a safe deposit box that you took your aunt to?"

"Her safe deposit box," Drake snapped.

"And you took her to the bank. Is that correct?"

"Yes."

"When you got to the bank, was there any money in that safe deposit box?"

"Yes."

"How much money was there?"

"Few thousand dollars."

"And what did you do with that money?"

"It's at her home. It's at my aunt's home."

"The money is at home?"

"At her house."

"Did you ever tell any authorities where that money was, such as the police?"

"No."

"During the time you lived with your aunt, did Mrs. Carrington ever come by to visit her?"

"Yes."

"Was your aunt angry or upset when Ms. Carrington would come by?"

"Yes."

"Why?"

"Danielle would harass her."

"She would harass her in front of you?"

"No."

"Who told you Mrs. Carrington was harassing your aunt?"

"She did, my auntie."

"Did you ever witness Mrs. Carrington harassing your aunt?"

"Personally?"

"Yes."

"The last time she was there."

"When was—?"

"Last time she was there, she brought two deputies with her, two police officers."

"Do you know why she brought the police officers with her?"

"No."

"And were you present during that meeting with the police officers?"

"Yes."

"Do you know whether or not the police officers were asking your aunt any questions in your presence?"

"No."

"So, in what way was Mrs. Carrington harassing Ms. Stanton by having that meeting with the police officers?"

"When I expressed to my auntie the deputies were there, okay, to assume that she's not being taken care of, and they're trying to put her in a convalescent home?"

"Did Mrs. Carrington ever tell you it was her intention to put your aunt in a convalescent hospital?"

"That's what I got from her."

"When did she tell you that?"

"She was putting her in there. That's why I got her."

"Was that a convalescent hospital or a rehabilitation hospital?"

"Convalescent home."

"Was that—?"

"Same thing. Rehabilitation. Convalescent. Okay, R and R Center," Drake said.

"But you never heard directly from Mrs. Carrington that it was her intention to put your aunt into a convalescent hospital. Did she ever tell you that?"

"She didn't have to tell me. She brought the police there," Drake barked.

"Have you been paying the bills for Ms. Stanton–your aunt– since you've been living there?"

"I sure do."

"And you've been paying the phone bill?"

"Yes."

"And do you write the checks for your aunt?"

"I write the checks out of my account."

"And how does your aunt give you the money to pay those bills?"

"They come out of my account."

"Did your aunt reimburse you the money that you've paid out?"

"No."

Judge Silverman jumped in. "Mr. Black, you live with your aunt. So is there any way she can live by herself, in your opinion?"

"She can't live by herself."

"She needs day-to-day care?" the judge asked.

"Yes. She needs care, not from some stranger. She needs care from her family, and I'm her family. And I will live with her and be her protector and take care of her as long as she lives. Because I love her."

"I don't doubt it. You are aware, like I said, that the trust documents and the power of attorney exist empowering your sister," the judge said.

"Sir, can I give you this?" Drake tried to hand the judge a paper.

"You can show me something if you show it to Mr. Barnes first. We have to show it to Mr. Barnes."

"Whatever you have to do, sir. I didn't know this man was going to be here."

"Just give him a second to look at it. I don't think he'll mind my seeing it."

The bailiff handed a copy of a living trust to me and Mr. Barnes. I got a glimpse of it, and one thing stood out on the page. Drake had named himself as the *Sole Beneficiary* of a bogus living trust. What in the world was he trying to do now? How would this affect the judge's decision?

"What is it?" the judge asked.

"I have been made the trustee of my aunt's estate," Drake said.

Attorney Barnes moved in. "Dated October 1, 2004, your honor."

"What's the date on the power of attorney?" the judge asked.

"September, I think twenty-first, 2004," I said.

"Well, I mean, if Mrs. Carrington can go and bring Ms. Stanton her power of attorney, then I don't see why Mr. Black can't bring his at the same time. To establish that if Ms. Stanton is incapacitated, who will handle her affairs. Is that correct? Has a doctor, to the best of your knowledge, declared your aunt to be incapacitated?"

"No, sir," Drake said.

"No. As of yet, you don't need to take these powers. Correct?"

"No, sir." Drake said.

"The power of attorney that also exists—is that just automatic—?"

"It's automatic," Attorney Barnes said.

"Right."

"It's effective immediately," Attorney Barnes said.

"So," the judge continued, addressing Drake, "while you have those powers, if she's incapacitated, your sister has been granted her powers at any time. All right. Now, I didn't do that, Mr. Black. That's just the documents I've been presented with. So this court is not to terminate those documents. Do you have anything else as regards harassment that you feel your sister has—"

"I feel as though my sister remaining away from my auntie would be the most important thing. That's what we came here to see if we could have the opportunity to make sure she doesn't come around her and cause problems."

"Okay. Thank you. You may step down," Judge Silverman said.

When Drake stepped down, I realized what a joke he had been. What could Drake do next?

* * *

Some months after the hearing, Juniper called me. Juniper was Drake's ex-wife. Drake had made her out to be the monster from hell all the years they had been married, and I believed him. Somehow, she and Drake had become friendly after their divorce, and she had been around since the day Drake moved into Lucille's house. Now Juniper was calling me. She told me exactly what had happened at the court hearing. She said she didn't want any part of it, but came to make sure Lucille was all right. This was too puzzling for even Einstein to figure out.

"You know, Lucille and Drake were sitting in the hallway waiting to go into the courtroom. That's when Isabelle and her daughter Marjorie showed up. Drake looked surprised, and whispered, "I wonder what they're doing here?" He then turned to them and asked, "What are you doing here?"

"I've come to defend my aunt's honor," Isabelle answered.

"You guys shouldn't be here?" Drake barked.

Juniper continued. "Isabelle and Marjorie looked at me and assumed I was with Lucille. We exchanged 'hello.'"

Juniper said that when Drake saw Isabelle and Marjorie, he knew somebody other than me wanted his neck. He was mad that they had come down there. He felt like he was being ambushed.

"What you guys doing here?" he asked.

"We're here to honor our aunt," Isabelle said.

After that exchange, Juniper said Isabelle and Marjorie entered the courtroom, while she, Drake, and Lucille followed.

Drake had brought a tape recorder to the courthouse to record Lucille. Juniper said Drake seemed totally oblivious to the fact that there were hundreds of people watching him. So, in view of the whole world, he asked Lucille questions, and she answered into the tape recorder.

"Who do you want to live with?" he asked, and recorded.

"I want to live with Drake," Lucille said.

"Who do you want your money and house to go to?"

"I want Drake to have everything I got."

After that, Drake rolled Lucille's wheelchair into the courtroom, hoping she would remember the drills.

Juniper said she remained outside, stunned.

After Drake testified, he came running out of the courtroom, grinning. "I think I won this."

Juniper said nothing, but decided to go into the courtroom to see what was happening.

* * *

There was a quiet rumbling in the courtroom because no one expected what the judge had just done. I mean no one. When the judge said the power of attorney signed by Aunt Lucille named me, Danielle, as the person to take care of her in the event she could not care for herself, the judge made it clear that the court could not make a determination on the two trusts. The judge paused.

"For now," the judge said, "based on the evidence and circumstances, I'm going to send Ms. Stanton home with Mrs. Carrington."

I gasped. I couldn't believe it. She was going home with me. I made my way over to Lucille, who was still sitting in her wheelchair at the courtroom table. I kissed her on the forehead, and said, "Sweetie, you're going home with me, okay?"

She had a bewildered look on her face. "Okay."

Juniper bolted from the courtroom out into the hallway, where Drake was sitting.

"I don't think you won this," she said, as we walked out.

"Oh, yeah."

The courtroom bailiff walked into the hallway. Drake tried to smile and chat with the bailiff. "How does the judge rule in these cases?"

"All depends on the statements."

Six sheriff's deputies assumed positions around Juniper and Drake.

"What's going on here?" Drake asked.

Silence fell on the cold floor. No one said a word.

Drake approached Lucille, trying to talk to her.

"Get back. Get back, sir. You can't approach them."

We continued walking, surrounded by our protectors, those six deputies.

Drake barked at Juniper, "Go and ask them for your niece's wheelchair."

"No, where would that leave Lucille?" Juniper asked.

When we were safely in the SUV, the deputies returned to the courthouse. Today my family was inextricably changed. We'd never be the same!

Chapter 26

I was sweating bullets by then. Another dilemma! My sweaty palms revealed the stress stirring inside me. Where was Aunt Lucille going to sleep? Who was going to give up their bed? I was trying to handle that situation, but right then I felt weak in the knees.

The weight of what had happened in court today was beyond belief. It was the move I had prayed for, the great thrust Lucille needed. Yet, it was both a blessing and a curse. My life was turning helter-skelter. I had to take off work to get Lucille set up. I didn't mind. It was just a temporary confusion for the good of my aunt.

When the judge came off the bench to talk with Lucille, I saw the sad look in her eyes. It was a glimpse into her disappointed heart. He seemed to know that her mind had lost its capacity to take her life out of harm's way. Who besides the judge could have done what he did?

Clearly, Judge Silverman sympathized with Lucille. She looked so frail and needy. Not that she was dressed inappropriately. I think what happened had to do more with what the judge saw beyond outer appearances. Lucille's eyes told a different story from what the feisty woman on the witness stand had said. The judge was the only one who could be her advocate. Certainly I couldn't have advocated for her, as Lucille had been tricked into rejecting me for Drake.

As we drove toward home, my mind rolled back to what had happened to turn the tide. I hadn't seen it coming, as Lucille's testimony had favored Drake over me. I just thought it was over. I knew that her desire for a safe, pleasant old age and fulfilled wishes had been destroyed. My mind replayed the scene, over and over, but I didn't see the sign of the judge's decision.

Then my thoughts turned to making Lucille comfortable for as long as she lived. That, too, was a colossal commitment.

My husband assured me that everything would work out. We put our heads together and came up with a plan. Lucille could sleep in our daughter Brooke's bedroom. She wasn't home from work to give consent, so we prayed that she wouldn't be too upset. Lucille needed to feel comfortable, warm and fuzzy, and, above all, protected.

We got home in the late afternoon, and I got busy feeding Lucille some fresh chicken noodle soup. She ate heartily. Then I left her and pulled out fresh linen for her new place to sleep. What good had come from Judge Silverman's decision? The first thing was that Lucille was out of danger. She had been moved to a strange place, but the strange place would provide comfort and safety. Now there was no way Drake could get angry beyond his control and hit her, which I thought he might ultimately have done. He couldn't curse her anymore. The judge had removed her from the place where she was being cursed at, which was beyond any woman's human dignity to endure.

When Brooke walked in from work, I wasn't sure how she would react. I rushed to get the news out. "Brooke, Judge Silverman sent Aunt Lucille home with us today. It was the—"

"Why?"

"I believe he knew she was in the worst possible environment. I think he decided that when he learned that Drake had cursed at her. I think he knew she was going to have no money to live on in a couple of months if Drake was allowed to keep putting her money into his account and spend it like pouring water."

"Well,' she shrugged, "if I have to give up my bed, I will."

"Thanks for not stressing me out over my decision. It happened in a second. Please help me change the linen."

"Okay, mom."

"You'll be blessed for this."

I went to the living room and assisted Lucille into Brooke's room. "Aunt Lucille, this is Brooke's bed, but she says you're welcome to sleep in it. Okay?"

Lucille looked at Brooke, who stood in front of her and said, "Thank you, baby."

"You're welcome."

"Danielle, can I lay down? I'm just plain tired."

"You sure can. Come on, I'll help you take your shoes off."

After a short nap, Lucille got up and looked around her safe but strange new place. "Danielle, that's a good little old sleeping bed."

"Good, Aunt Lucille. I'm glad you could rest. You don't have any clothes or any personal things here, other than what you're wearing."

"What I'm gonna do?"

"We're going to get some of your personal things from your house."

"Okay. When we going?"

My husband Spencer called his brother Lance, who is a peace officer. Lance agreed to ride with us. I wasn't looking for any more trouble with Drake of any kind, and this precaution was just in case. Just before dusk, Lance arrived and I introduced him to Lucille. I wanted her to feel protected, not fearful of him.

"Aunt Lucille, this is Lance, Spencer's brother. He's going with us to your house. Okay?"

"Okay."

"Let me get your sweater."

"Okay."

We piled into the SUV, and the ride resembled going to a wake. Everyone was somber, dreading to meet up with Drake.

I wondered what we would experience. Lucille hadn't been home since she left her house that morning. I was also wondering if her heart might start to long for familiar surroundings when she got there, ignoring the fact that Judge Silverman had possibly saved her life. She might start crying and holding on. But who knew where her things were, better than she?

Maybe Drake wouldn't be there. I could use such a blessing right about now! When we arrived, I turned to a blank-faced Aunt Lucille. I couldn't read her.

"Aunt Lucille, we're at your house to get some of your things."

"Okay, Danielle."

She reached for the car door.

"Wait just a minute. Spencer's going to help you out," I said.

We made our way to the walkway and up those menacing steps. Lucille leaned on Spencer for support. I had gone ahead of them with the duffle bag that I had taken from the car. Lance followed closely behind. It all felt surreal! Just like someone had died.

I rang the doorbell, hoping no one would answer, but Drake answered. What about the blessing if he wasn't there? Scratch that!

"We've come for Aunt Lucille's personal belongings." I tried to sound strong.

He reluctantly unlocked the door, and we walked in. I spotted Juniper near the swinging kitchen door, and I made my way toward Lucille's bedroom. Before I got any further than the dining room adjacent to the living room, I saw that Drake had bolted to the hallway. He grabbed hold of Aunt Lucille, peeling her away from Spencer. Lance was standing nearby, observing. Drake began to grovel in front of Lucille.

"Auntie, you don't have to leave this house. This is your house. Don't you want to stay here? You don't have to leave."

Unless I were in another place this morning and didn't hear the judge's ruling, I wouldn't believe what Drake was asking. He was asking her to break the judge's ruling.

He turned to me and blurted out, "Danielle, Aunt Lucille ain't going nowhere with you."

His comment must have been based on a senior who had been whittled into submission to him. "Don't you want to stay here?" He asked Lucille.

I turned on a dime. "She's not staying here!"

"This is her house."

"She's not staying."

"Who said?"

"The judge said."

Drake went from one degree of mania to another. Lucille sat in her old familiar green folding chair, while he got louder and louder. She seemed mentally detached from everything, as if she were saying, "Hurry up and let's go."

Drake stormed into the bedroom. "You the smart one. You made us all your servants."

While pulling things from Lucille's dresser drawer, I yelled back, "You have zero character. That's your problem." Drake blocked me so I couldn't get into the closet. He had lost his mind!

"Drake, you'd better move."

"If you want to get in, climb over the bed."

My knees trembled. Sharp pain shot through them, but I climbed over the bed. Juniper moved near the bedroom door. "Danielle, can I help you find anything."

"No, but thanks."

Juniper turned to Drake. "Leave her alone and let her get Aunt Lucille's things."

Drake kept blocking me. "Drake, I don't have to take this bullying from you. If you don't move out of my way, I'm calling the police."

He must have thought I was kidding. He didn't move, and I charged to the telephone in the hallway and dialed 911. Out of my peripheral vision, I saw Lance standing in a menacing pose, observing. I gave the operator the information, and then made my way back to Lucille's bedroom. Drake cleared the closet door. I grabbed a few things, including her medicine bottles. The sleeping pill bottle was missing.

I didn't ask Drake about the pills. I stuffed the duffle bag without asking Lucille what to take, or what she felt most comfortable in. I started toward the living room just as Juniper left the bedroom, too. She stopped in the hallway and spoke to Spencer and Lance about what happened in court. They kept their eyes on Drake.

Drake kept hurling insults from his bedroom, his anger escalating. I found myself embroiled in a full-fledged verbal assault with him. He was relentless. Spencer called from the hallway.

"Danielle, don't let Drake drag you into an argument. Hurry up and let's go."

I was so angry that I didn't even hear Spencer. I had made my way into the living room when Spencer walked in and brought me back to reality. "This is not what you want to do." He shook his head.

On that sour note, we moved towards the front door, Lucille in tow. We left Drake groveling, as he rushed into the living room.

"Aunt Lucille, this is your house. You don't have to go."

We ignored him. I heard him cursing as we walked to the car.

* * *

Many months later, I was going to work in our home office when the phone rang. It was 9 o'clock in the morning.

"Danielle, girl, this is Juniper. I've been trying to reach you, but I didn't have your phone number."

I was shocked. What did she possibly want to say to me? I

couldn't imagine. Did she want to plead innocence and tell me she had nothing to do with the lawsuit? I made a deal with myself to hear what she had to say. She elaborated on how she got my phone number from a friend of mine who knew her casually.

"I want to tell you everything. How Drake mistreated Aunt Lucille with those sleeping pills. How he talked to her. Just everything." She was crying by then.

"Okay. I'm listening." It was over, so why did she feel this explanation was necessary?

"When you returned to Aunt Lucille's to get some of her things, and after I had left the room, Drake went to the vanity table and picked up five one-hundred dollar bills. He offered me one." Her voice broke. "I asked him to give it to you since Aunt Lucille was going to be living with you."

"Oh," I said.

"He asked me if I wanted some."

"What did you say?" I asked.

"I said, 'no way.'"

"He took out his money clip and attached the bills."

"Umm," I said, skeptical of her motives.

"I have some more to tell you, but I'll call you later."

"Okay."

Surely, Drake knew it was time to move out of Lucille's house! That situation loomed over me—him living in her house. That was another battle that had to be fought.

Chapter 27

It had been a week since Lucille came to stay in our home and I had taken one giant step—setting an appointment with ACAN Health Care Agency. Today, they were scheduled to visit and see how they could assist me with Lucille's care. It was the same agency that I arranged to visit when she lived in her home, and Drake ran the representative away. When the doorbell rang, I knew it was ACAN. When I opened the door, a smiling middle-aged woman in a navy cotton suit stood there.

"Hello, my name is Margaret. I'm from ACAN Agency."

"Come in and let me introduce you to my aunt. Her name is Lucille."

"Okay."

"Lucille, this is Margaret. She's from the Home Health Agency at ACAN and she'll be spending some time with you."

"Okay."

"Okay, Margaret. Lucille loves to play cards. And, in addition, she'll need assistance with getting her food. Sometimes she can feed herself. You'll just have to ask her if she feels like it."

"Okay."

"And, oh, she'll need help when taking her bath."

"Do you have a shower or a tub?"

"Actually I have both, but she prefers the shower."

"That's fine."

"Come this way, and let me show you where the bathroom is and where her room is."

"Alright."

I was thinking to myself, this is going to be great because it will free me up to take care of my own and my family's business. I had wanted to do this for a long time.

"And remember, Margaret, she loves to play cards."

"That's fine with me."

"She's probably ready to play a hand or two right now."

The moment was so hopeful that it reminded me of Lucille back in the day. She and Nat loved to entertain. Lucille could cut a rug dancing. She was the apple of Nat's eye and dancing with Nat sent her into ecstasy. But, as much as she loved dancing, playing cards had to be a hundred times better.

I wanted her to taste those times I saw her happy again, and other times she told me about when I was a girl. When Nat wasn't working on the railroad, their house was the spot for entertaining. Many lasting friendships were born out of those card-playing dates. That beautiful maple table was worn ragged from slapping down of cards when the winner announced victory. Lucille prepared a feast and treated her guests like kings and queens. Something about card parties made her feel great.

"Do you want to play cards with me?" Lucille asked Margaret.

"Okay." Margaret walked over to her and stroked her shoulder.

"Okay, the name of the game is *Pity Pat.* Do you know how to play?" Lucille asked.

"No, but I'm sure you'll teach me, right?"

"Yeah. It's real easy."

The nurse played the hand, and later confided to me that Lucille cheated by changing the rules as the game went along. Just to see Lucille mentally engaged was encouraging. As long as she kept her mind busy, she was better able to focus on mental tasks, such as remembering her name, where she lived, whose house it was, and the names of my husband and children. Lucille never forgot my name. She always knew who I was. That made me happy, because if she forgot me, then who was she going to remember? It was a critical time.

In late October 2004, Lucille was eating breakfast, her oatmeal dribbling, when she said, "When you gonna get Drake outta my house?"

I was shocked. "Lucille, what do you mean by that?"

"Well, if I'm not living in my house, he sure shouldn't be living in it."

She came across really clearly. It was amazing.

"You're right."

"Do you think he's tore up my house?"

Did she think he would destroy her property? Had he ever threatened that he would do that? What a statement from a person who, on some days, struggled just to participate in basic conversation.

"I don't think he's torn up your house." I sure hope not, I thought.

I didn't know because I hadn't been back to her house since the day we picked up her clothes. Furthermore, I had no intention of going back, as long as Drake lived there. The last thing I needed was to compound my worry load. I felt the old burden returning. I knew I'd have to get Drake out of the house if he hadn't already moved, which I doubted.

He probably thought he should be able to stay in Lucille's house as long as he wanted to. But the next day, I began eviction proceedings, and Lucille signed the papers.

I knew Drake was thinking it would be better to have him there, so the place didn't attract vagrants and thieves. But that wasn't going to happen. After four attempts to serve him, the processor found Drake on November 1. He was leaving the house at 7 o'clock in the morning. The server handed him a document— Notice to Vacate the Premises by December 1, 2004.

* * *

November 30, 2004: I got up early before everyone else to read my morning devotional. Almost that the same moment, the doorbell rang. I could see the reflection of two men on the other side. When I looked through the peek hole, Drake stood there along side the LA County Sheriff Deputy. What's this all about? I thought. I opened the door.

"Where's Lucille? I want to give her the keys," Drake said.

"She's asleep. I'll take them."

"You'll have to sign here." He handed me a form.

"Sign where?"

"Right there." Drake pointed to the bottom line on the form.

"Were you going to ask how your most beloved auntie is?" I asked him.

He smirked, rolled his eyes, and stalked off. As he was leaving, he turned and asked, "Where's the wheelchair? It belongs to Juniper's niece."

"Okay. I'll get it for you." Anything to get his abhorrent attitude out of my face. At that same moment, I sincerely asked God to forgive me.

"Dear God, please allow me to detest the character of sin, but to love my brother, a human being. Help me. Amen."

Chapter 28

November 3, 2004: I was faced with yet another Lucille dilemma—her sleeping pattern. She seemed to be worried that peaceful nights of sleep were gone forever. She finally seemed to understand the enormity of what stripped her of all her life's savings. She constantly repeated one phrase!

"Danielle, when you getting my money back from Drake?"

"Soon, Auntie Lucille."

I had no idea when we'd get a court date to address Drake's theft of Lucille's money. I was told it could take up to a year, or more.

Lately, Lucille had been showing signs of lapsing back into forgetfulness. It was hard to believe that just weeks before, she could rattle off, "When you goin' to court to get my money back?"

I felt so sorry that she had to go through so much. She deserved to know how and when she'd be made whole. So, for as many times as she'd ask, I prayed for the strength to patiently answer her. My family opened its arms to save Lucille from what looked like a life on the fast track to a bad end.

Now, Lucille was beginning to sleep all the time. She couldn't seem to keep her eyes open. Whenever she woke up, she would ask, "Danielle, can I go lay down?"

Soon, sleep would gather on her eyelids. To deny her sleep would be cruel. These days, it seemed that the overdose of sleeping pills had programmed her system to think of nights and days as pretty much the same. She was beginning to talk to herself. Her speech had become garbled. I was watching the entire downward spiral, and it was painful to watch.

As if my life couldn't get worse, it did! I was at my desk working, thinking that Lucille's situation was as bad as it could get. I encouraged myself by thinking— Just hang in there–things do have a way of working out. It sounded so noble. .

The doorbell rang, and I was served with another summons to appear in court! My eyes fell on—Appear on November 17, 2004. *Lucille isn't living at her home, so what could Drake possibly want?* It was difficult to press through the mist of such insanity. I opened the summons and read it.

I was livid. I declare, if that man ever channeled just half of the energy he puts into trying to destroy me, he might be redeemed, forgiven, and made whole. Then in a flash I saw it. The summons was Drake's way of dodging eviction papers, to stay in Lucille's home without paying rent.

On the morning of November 17, 2004, I headed to court again—to meet Drake's challenge. Spencer stayed home with Lucille. Why should I subject her to another round of torment? I was going by myself, but I wasn't going alone. God was with me.

I left home early because I didn't want to get caught on the 110 Freeway in early morning gridlock. As I drove in the patchy traffic, all I could think about was what could happen if I didn't make it to court on time. First of all, Drake would get his wish to win a baseless restraining order issued against me, denying me the right to go to Lucille's house for any reason. Just then,

I pulled into a parking lot near the courthouse and looked at the clock. It was only 7:45. I would make it inside in plenty of time.

I was deep in thought when a peddler tried to hand me a flyer. "Okay, Miss. Just want to offer you some help."

"No, thank you."

Thankfully, the line inside the courthouse moved swiftly. The next stop took me to the metal detector station. The beeper went off just because I was in the biggest hurry. But the sheriffs didn't care that I was in a hurry.

"Ma'am, would you please step over here."

"Okay." I stepped over there.

The officer passed the search wand over me, and I was cleared to enter the courtroom. I gathered myself, my things, and walked inside.

I looked for my attorney, but he hadn't arrived. Or, at least, I hadn't spotted him. I could only hope. I prayed that he hadn't forgotten. The day was going to be a defining moment for either Drake or me. When the proceedings ended today, somebody was going to be victorious. The question was who. Throwing in the proverbial towel was not an option. I had responsibilities hanging over me, and quitting now would be disastrous for too many people, not least of all, Lucille.

I walked outside the courtroom, looking for my attorney, but he was nowhere in sight. Then I dialed his office. "Hi, my name is Danielle Carrington, and I was to meet Attorney Barnes at the courthouse this morning."

"Yes, Mrs. Carrington, Mr. Barnes is scheduled to appear there today. Would you like his cell phone number?"

"That would be great."

When I dialed his cell phone, Attorney Barnes answered.

"I'm sorry. The traffic is so bad, but I'll be there before court begins."

"Okay."

After speaking with my attorney, I felt my anxiety level go way down. I made my way back into the courtroom and found a seat toward the back, where I could wait for Attorney Barnes. I contemplated the possibilities that could happen with my opponents; yet I was hopeful that all would go well. Finally, Attorney Barnes rushed in and found me in the back.

"Danielle, I apologize again for being late. Traffic was a dog."

"I was just hoping you hadn't forgotten." I settled down.

Drake and Juniper arrived, and took seats in the row just behind me and my attorney. I turned my head slightly, and could see Drake sitting directly behind us. It felt as if he were breathing on the back of my neck. It was very uncomfortable. I whispered to my attorney, and we moved two seats down.

That felt better. Soon, the court called the case of Drake Black vs. Danielle Carrington. "Would the parties please stand. Do you both swear to tell the truth, the whole truth, and nothing but the truth, so help you God."

"I do."

Drake swore, "I do."

Oomph, I thought. Does Drake know what the truth means? He had sworn to tell the truth at the last hearing, but he had straight out lied without a blink. So what would make this time any different?

"Your honor, I would like to have the case continued so I can retain legal counsel," Drake said.

"What?" I asked.

"Mr. Black, you knew you were coming here today, didn't you?" Judge Lowe asked.

"Yes, ma'am," he answered.

"And you have had plenty of time to retain legal counsel," Judge Lowe said.

"Yes, but—" Drake started.

"Mr. Black, I'm going to have to deny your request to continue this case."

Drake's face dropped. He had come there representing himself. I read somewhere that "A man is a fool who has himself as a lawyer." Drake's request prompted the judge to stare at him. Then the judge eyed something on the computer screen.

What in particular is the judge targeting? I thought.

"Mr. Black, have you ever filed an action in court against Danielle Carrington before?"

"Yes," Drake answered.

"Okay, Mr. Black, I see, according to the minutes of the court, you were here on October nineteenth. Is that correct?"

"Yes."

"And because you didn't get the ruling you wanted, you filed another action against Danielle Carrington three days later, on October 22, 2004. Is this correct?"

"Yes."

"And that second request brings you here today. Is this correct?"

"Your honor, she filed a police report accusing me of stealing my auntie's money."

"Well, Mr. Black, was she in charge of your aunt's affairs?"

"Yes."

"Well, she did the right thing. If she hadn't done that, she would be in trouble. Mr. Black, I have never done this before, in all my days on the bench. But I think you abused the court system by filing again. I order you to pay Danielle Carrington's court fees, and you filed another allegation."

I was stunned, but pleased. Drake looked as if a heavyweight champion had punched him on the side of his head.

"Attorney Barnes, how much are your hourly fees?"

"Three hundred fifty dollars an hour, Your Honor."

"Mr. Black, I order you to pay Mrs. Carrington's attorney fees for two hours at the rate of three-hundred and fifty dollars an hour, for a total amount of seven hundred dollars," the judge ordered. "Do you understand, Mr. Black?"

"Yes."

"Further, Mr. Black, these fees are payable at the rate of one hundred dollars per month for the next seven months. If you miss a payment, the entire amount becomes due and payable," Judge Lowe ruled. "Are there any questions."

No one said a word. What was there to say?

"If there's nothing else, the parties are excused."

The judge had just dealt Drake a taste-of-his-own-medicine blow.

I waited until Drake had left the courtroom and then proceeded to my car. Indeed, God did what He promised He would do–protect me! Even so, I wondered what Drake Black would do to strike again!

Chapter 29

I sat in my kitchen, imagining the rich buttery smells I used to experience in there, comparing that to the many months of harsh battle with Drake. Lucille had died two weeks before, and my grief was poignant and deep. The family members gathered for her services and prayed for special deliverance of her soul to a place of peace and protection. But some members of the family didn't come. It was a somber day, cloudy and cool, and lonely. It was a day when the suffering and death had lost its sting, though—somewhat. Much of the grief was numbed by so much debris left to be cleaned up.

I was still trying to deal with the entire disturbance surrounding Lucille's death. I had been trying to bring her home from the convalescent home so that she could die in the warmth and comfort of home, and not in the cold but caring place where she finally breathed her last breath. Drake had always accused me of threatening to put Lucille in a nursing home, like the time when the police came to Lucille's house after Drake stole her money. I could still hear him yelling, "Lucille, Danielle's trying to put you in a convalescent home!"

Lucille hated the very idea of that ever happening. She had lived in her home for more than 50 years, and by all accounts, she wanted to die there. But, near the end of her life, when she was admitted to a convalescent home, it was not because of me. It was because she had been beaten down financially, and emotionally. Some family members even believed she was abused physically. Those menacing sleeping pills that Drake gave her when she was in his custody seemed to thrust her into a downward spiral by the time she came to live with me.

I wondered if Drake remotely considered that he was part of the reason Lucille ended up in a convalescent home? Anyway, I was grieving that I couldn't lift her when she could no longer get up. The aide couldn't lift her daily. Still, I grieved that she had to leave this world in a place that was against her wishes.

Taking Drake to court was going to be a monumental task unlike anything I had ever tackled. But, up to this point, God had been good to me and I didn't doubt for a minute that He would see me through. So, my thoughts were embroiled in what all of this really meant.

The phone rang. When I answered, I didn't quite know what to think. On the other end of the line was a woman's voice saying, "I'm Miss Scotty."

"Miss who?"

"Miss Scotty."

"Who are you?"

"I'm Lucille's neighbor."

"Where do you live?"

"About four doors from Lucille."

"In the same block?"

"Yes."

"How can I help you?"

"I just wanted you to know that Drake Black stole money from Lucille."

Now, my mind went into another tailspin. First of all, who was this woman, how did she get my phone number, and what ax did she have to grind with me or Drake? But I listened.

"I just want you to know—"

"Know what?"

"I just want you to know that Drake Black stole thousands of dollars from Lucille."

"And how do you know that?"

"Because I seen the money."

"Uh huh."

"I know Drake mistreated Lucille."

Now why would this person call me? Did this mean there was somebody involved in this mess who actually had a conscience? What finally caused her to pick up the phone and dial my number? Or, rather, had Drake been bragging to people about the money he stole?

"He stole all the money in the house."

Now, how could she know this without Drake telling her? Other than Drake, there were only a few of us who knew about the money in the house, and she sure didn't get the information from any of us. So, I had to conclude that in some deluded state, Drake told her about the money in the house.

"Why are you calling me?"

"Because injustice is been done."

The word *injustice* struck me. It had been done. She was right, though, I was dreading another battle. I still didn't say too much because I preferred that she talk rather than me asking her questions.

"Drake's got thousands of dollars."

"How do you know?"

"He offered me some money."

I restrained myself from asking her whether she had taken any of it. I didn't want to know. What good would knowing that do for me? Was she going to return the money if she had taken some of it? I didn't know what she would have done, but right now it was a moot issue!

Lucille was dead and gone from the burdens of this world. That fact almost gave me a sense of relief.

"He's been traveling a lot." She emphasized the words "a lot." "And he's putting new carpet in the house."

Now, I was thinking, when did this house become Drake's to begin a remodeling? He had been evicted. Who gave him permission to do any of that? Who gave him permission to move back into the house? He had been lawfully evicted. Some legal mind must have given him that poor advice. Then I recalled he had that bogus trust that he must have convinced himself was legally binding.

The court date to determine the validity of the two trusts was fast approaching. It had not died. After that court date, it would no longer be an issue which trust would be valid, and which one would be bogus. The court would have the final word. The end, at last, would come to this seemingly 100-year war. I would be free, whether I had vindicated the final years of Lucille's misery or not. For certain, I had tried.

Chapter 30

June 6, 2005: Dear God, I have another big problem. It seems that's all I get these days when I'm dealing with something connected to Drake. Now the investigators haven't been able to serve Drake with court papers because they can't find him. This can't be. Not after all of this. Would you please find him, Lord? Danielle kept writing while sitting in the chair next to the bed.

It was a beautiful summer day. From my yard, I felt the warmth of the glowing sun beaming down, but it took on that distant feeling of pending winter. Although my attorney had announced that Drake couldn't be found, I just stood there and smiled. I knew that giving up and giving in was not an option, not with the torment still stirring inside of me. I recalled the conversation I had with my attorney.

"What do you mean, the investigators can't find Drake? Did he fall off the face of the earth?"

I didn't want to consider the extreme possibility that if Drake couldn't be found, he couldn't be served, and if he couldn't be served, the case was closed. That wouldn't work. I took a seat on the patio and shook my head in frustration. I began to cry, wondering how that could happen.

I wondered why investigators trained to locate people in the farthest corner of the world couldn't find Drake Black. No, I had to change my attitude. I had to use my faith. My faith could find Drake and bring him to justice. He couldn't have fallen off the end of the earth. My head throbbed. Before this ordeal, I never had headaches or high blood pressure. I always had perfect blood pressure, 120/76. Now, my doctor had diagnosed me as having high blood pressure, enough to require medication. Oh, my headache!

My mind kept replaying thoughts, like a broken record. If the investigators said they couldn't find Drake, how many times have they tried? How many places have they looked? Did they comb Los Angeles and all the surrounding cities? They must have given up prematurely. I had invested too much money, time, and health in this to let it go. And what kind of message would that send to Drake? I had to find a way to let Drake know the court date had been set, and he was expected to be there. His bogus trust had to be annulled, or he would have the ultimate victory—Lucille's home. He would own her home. After all he did to her.

Preparation for the trial had involved a massive amount of e-mailing, faxing, and phone calls. Spending all of that time told me I must move forward. Drake, you will be found. I don't know when, but you will be found, I thought.

I was sorry I didn't have the papers with me when my sister and I went to Lucille's to change the locks. That would have worked perfectly. But, as I thought about it, we didn't have a court date at that time. And my mind was playing games with me.

* * *

November 14, 2005: I remember the date as if it were yesterday. As a matter of fact, I shall never forget that defining moment for as long as I live. It was a moment that stood out like no other.

On Saturdays I usually went to the post office and took my car to be washed. While waiting, I decided to walk across the street to the bank. Each Saturday, that's exactly what I did, except that day, I changed the order. I felt the strong presence of God and felt like going to the post office first. I decided to wait for my car and then drive, not walk, to the bank. I didn't know why I felt it was necessary to change the order of my normal routine, but I didn't question it. I just obeyed.

While I waited for my car, a gentleman came and sat beside me. I didn't look up and pay particular attention to him. Shortly, the car wash attendant signaled me. I gathered my things, got up, and walked to my car. As I was getting into the car, the man sitting next to me came over. I felt a little nervous, and moved a bit faster. I handed the attendant my claim check and a tip. The gentleman came closer.

"Danielle, Danielle?" he called.

I whirled around and noticed that the man was a cousin I hadn't seen in five or six years.

"Hi, Danielle, I didn't know that was you."

"Hi, Glenn. How are you?" I asked.

"I'm fine. How about you? When's the last time you spoke with Drake?" he asked.

"Well, I haven't spoken with him in quite some time," I said, with skepticism. Glenn must have heard something about the upcoming trial. So I would keep everything close to my chest. I didn't want to send up any red flags.

"When I last spoke with him, I asked him about your mother. How's she doing?"

What does he know? I wondered.

"She's got a disease that affects her ability to walk, but otherwise she's doing pretty good."

"You been by to see your brother lately?"

"No, I haven't seen him for some time," I said nonchalantly. This couldn't be happening, could it?

"You ought to drop by and see him. He lives right down the street from me. Let's see: 2701 South Hampton Avenue. Yeah, apartment number four."

Everything in me stood still. He had just told me where Drake was. The person the investigators couldn't find. It had just happened. I needed a pen and paper, but I dared not look like I needed it. I didn't want to let on that the information he had just given me was like receiving the golden egg. I was beyond ecstatic. I tempered my ecstasy and celebrated in my heart. I was hoping the grey matter in my brain would hold the information long enough for me to get to a pencil and a place to write it down.

"Glenn, it was so good to see you. Tell your wife I said hi. Take care of yourself."

I started my car, pulled around the corner, stopped, pulled a pen and paper from my purse, and wrote down the address in a hurry. I couldn't wait to call my attorney. The hotshot investigators could not find Drake, but Divine Intervention had. Everything in the dark comes to the light. God unearthed Drake through a most unlikely source.

Chapter 31

May 30, 2006: Dear God, thank you for finding Drake. You can do exceedingly abundantly above all I can think or ask. Danielle wrote from her favorite chair beside the bed.

When Drake was served the summons to appear, I heard from his friend that he told everybody what a demon I was. I didn't respond. I just didn't care. The date for the deposition was upon us. It was the last event leading up to the trial. I knew that the bogus living trust was going to be found out, somehow. "Truth always prevails," I mumbled to myself.

Drake and his attorney, Ora Mae Duffy, subpoenaed Dr. Donoghue to appear. They were the ones he called for the deposition to prove that Lucille was mentally stable enough to sign that bogus trust. My attorney, Elliott Spillinger, was also present. Elliott Spillinger, the tall Jewish lawyer I had used for the past few months, cleared his throat. He lifted his glasses and pulled on his ear, looking and listening intently. He was all business, as usual. Dr. Donoghue was already on the witness stand.

"What is your profession?" Drake's attorney asked.

"I am a medical doctor with a specialty in neurology," Dr. Donoghue answered.

"Do you remember treating a patient by the name of Lucille Stanton?"

"Yes. She came in complaining of numbness in her right hand. This numbness had been present for several months. Her niece told me there had been a problem of memory loss. Up until a few months before I saw her, she had been able to live by herself. Other living arrangements became necessary because she was discovered sitting in a bathtub where, according to the niece, she had been for two days. The patient was hospitalized at Mayfair Medical following the incident."

"Now, that report, where it says, 'Examination'—" Attorney Duffy said.

"Yes, ma'am," Dr. Donoghue answered.

"It says, 'The patient was awake and alert.' Is that correct?"

"That's correct."

"And she was cooperative? Would you like a copy of this?"

My attorney, Elliott Spillinger, turned to Attorney Duffy and said, "Whatever we are reading from, a copy should be attached to the deposition so that we all know what document we are referring to."

I wasn't present at the deposition hearing, but when I later read over the transcript, I thought, doesn't Drake's attorney know protocol? There is procedure to follow when deposing individuals. All parties are supposed to have copies of everything presented. That was so basic.

"Okay. Do you want to identify the document you are reading, doctor?" Attorney Duffy asked.

"This is an outpatient neurological consultation."

"Now, you say a Mini Mental Status Exam was 14/30. What does that mean?"

"Well, there is a standard exam given in doctors' offices with 30 questions that the patient has to answer. We have normal scores for various age groups, and in her age group, a normal score would probably be anything above 26. This exam is heavily weighted toward language functions."

"So more language than mental?" Attorney Duffy asked.

"No, ma'am. Language is a mental function. It's a cognitive function. But the exam, the Mini Mental Status Exam, tests several different cognitive functions, and they are mostly related to language," Dr. Donoghue said.

"And the 14/30 rating, how does that rate on your scale?" Attorney Duffy asked.

"That indicates the patient is moderately to severely impaired cognitively," Dr. Donoghue said.

"Okay. Down at the bottom on number one, it says, 'Probable senile dementia of the Alzheimer's type.'"

"Yes, ma'am."

"The next document you are looking at, could you identify it for the record?"

"This is a radiology report from Los Cabana Imaging Center, and it's a radiology report of a brain CT scan, given without any dye or without contrast as the report indicates."

"And what was the outcome of that?" Attorney Duffy asked.

"The report indicated that there were areas in the brain, on both sides of the brain, that were indicative of small vessel disease. This is not the way they describe it, but I'm going to describe it for you, put it differently."

"Thank you."

"Small vessel disease involving the brain, it's a common finding, especially in elderly patients, and it could be in varying degrees. In her case, they said that it was patchy, which I took to mean that it was not confluent. In other words, you didn't see it everywhere you looked in the white matter of the brain, but it was there in a patchy fashion."

"Go on, doctor."

"So this is a nonspecific finding. Their conclusion was periventricular. That means it's surrounding the ventricles of the brain. These are fluid-filled spaces and deep inside the brain, part of the normal anatomy. So these changes in the blood vessels are located around these ventricles, which are a typical area for their location."

"Does this particular exam determine the mental ability of a patient?" Attorney Duffy asked.

"No, it does not!" Dr. Donoghue said

"Does that have any reference to her mental state or her ability to think?"

"That's a very controversial issue. The way I usually deal with this is, if I see these types of changes and they are widespread and confluent–in other words, they are not there in sort of a hit-and-miss fashion, they are not patchy–then, under those circumstances, I think that's when it's so severe that it actually can affect mental function in a patient. Where it's patchy like this, it's less conclusive, and I really could not make any statement as to the significance or the relationship of this finding to the patient's mental status or cognitive abilities. I could not make any connection with any reasonable degree of medical probability."

"You said it was inconclusive as to whether or not she had Alzheimer's, is that correct?" Attorney Duffy asked.

"No, I didn't say that with regard to this report. What I said with regard to this report is that it's inconclusive as to whether the degree of small vessel disease had any effect on her cognitive function. Whether the amount that was present was sufficient to affect her cognitive function, I was unable to conclude one way or another. I did not say anything about Alzheimer's."

"You did prescribe some medication?" she probed.

"Yes, I did. My report, I believe, states that I prescribed a medication that is called Aricept."

"Could you tell us what's the purpose of the Aricept?" Attorney Duffy inquired.

"The main purpose of the Aricept in a patient with a moderately advanced disease like this is to try to improve the patient's behavior and manageability. It's also used to help improve memory, but in patients who are in the early stages of Alzheimer's or who are in the pre-Alzheimer's stage of what they call mild cognitive impairment. I would not expect to see much in the way of improvement of memory, but I'm hoping to see more improvement in terms of behavior and manageability of the patient."

"Getting back to the notes, what does that say at the bottom there?" Attorney Duffy asked.

"Where it says, 'Impression' from the top line?" Dr. Donoghue asked

"Read the whole thing for us, please."

Dr. Donoghue located the spot and read. "Probable right carpal tunnel. And beneath that it says, 'SDAT-MMSE 14/30.'"

"Now, a person with a score of 14/30, do you think that they could read and understand what they were reading?"

Dr. Donoghue was noncommittal. "Sometimes they can and sometimes they can't."

"And would that be the same answer to understanding when someone is reading to them?"

"Yes, ma'am."

"Anywhere in your notes that you show where you actually diagnosed her with Alzheimer's disease yourself?"

Dr. Donoghue seemed unable to follow Attorney Duffy's logic. "May I answer your question with a question for clarification's sake?"

"Yes, sir."

"Do you mean a definitive diagnosis?"

"Yes."

"I never made a definitive diagnosis of Alzheimer's."

She looked bewildered. "And did you make a definitive diagnosis of any dementia?"

"Yes."

"And what type of dementia?" she asked.

"Well, the diagnosis of dementia   dementia is sort of a generic term that is really not a diagnosis. It's really a one-word statement of a patient's condition, and it means that the patient has cognitive dysfunction in more than one area, which the Mini Mental Status Exam results clearly show. You say the patient is demented and then you attempt to diagnose what type of dementia it is, which is what I did. I said, 'Probable senile dementia of the Alzheimer's type.'"

"Doctor, you said on this test, this Mini Mental Status Exam, that the rating was fourteen thirty."

"Yes."

"And you said that that was moderately severely impaired cognitively. Can you break that down into—"

"The term 'cognition' refers to higher brain function, which is unique to the human species. There are many realms of cognition that include judgment, language, just an example of recognition of faces, recognition of music, organization or tasks, the ability to perform tasks, the ability to program your muscle system to do what you want it to do. The ability to think and to reason. All of this falls under cognition."

"So, if it's moderately severely impaired, what does that mean?" Attorney Spillinger asked.

"Well, what that usually means is that the patient has advanced to–has advanced to the point where they really cannot be relied upon to care for themselves, so they have become dependent on others to care for them. In a patient with Alzheimer's disease, a lot of times they start to become socially withdrawn, will spend most of the day sitting around, sometimes watching TV, sometimes not. At this time, they can start to become delusional and hostile and can start to wander. They start to require assistance in what we refer to as activities of daily living, such as dressing oneself, bathing oneself, using the bathroom, feeding oneself."

"Is there some bell-shaped curve that the literature talks about in terms of a patient like this, when an onset is and how long it lasts and things of that nature? I realize it's different in each patient," Attorney Spillinger said.

"It is different, but on average, if this is a patient with senile dementia of the Alzheimer's type –" Dr. Donoghue paused a moment, then continued.

"In November 2004, if they scored in this range on the Mini Mental Status Exam, they have usually had the disorder for at least a couple of years," Dr. Donoghue advised.

"That's why I wanted to ask, did you conclude that she did have memory loss?" Duffy asked.

"You know, that's not obviously evident from my notes, but with this diagnosis and with the Mini Mental Status Exam, that would be my conclusion – that would have been my conclusion that she did have memory loss and that it was probably pretty severe."

"In November of 2004, did you conclude whether she could understand what she was reading? And if she could read, could she understand what she was reading?" Attorney Duffy asked.

"Again there is no documentation, but I would have con-cluded–I think I would have concluded that SHE WAS NOT CAPABLE OF MANAGING HER OWN PERSONAL OR FI-NANCIAL AFFAIRS."

"What about reading?" Attorney Spillinger asked.

"She might be able to read, but I'm not certain that she would be able to fully understand what she was reading."

"Thank you, Dr. Donoghue, for your time. You may step down."

The conclusion of that deposition didn't look good for Drake and his attorney. And the information given by Dr. Donoghue was the weapon Drake and his attorney would have to overcome. In other words, Lucille couldn't have known what she was reading at the time she signed the bogus trust. Further, she must have been coerced to do it.

Chapter 32

June 6, 2006: Spencer and I rushed into the courthouse, followed by our daughter Brooke and our son Travis. We got in the line leading into the Royal Courts of Justice. We were almost at the front door when the line suddenly stopped.

What was happening? There were so many security measures–officers with wands and doors with beepers and conveyor belts on which to place our "life stories" as we emptied out our pockets and purses. I peeked around the crowd and saw a woman struggling clumsily to put her "life story" back in her purse. I wished she'd hurry, as I couldn't be late. Today, the court would determine which one of the trusts is bogus and which one is real.

The trial was blocking everything else from my mind. Trial. Trial. Trial. The trial was all I could see, think of, and anticipate. I closed my eyes and took a deep breath. Injustice was coming to a conclusion. Being wiped out, I kept thinking that whatever you do has a payoff, good or bad, and before the wipe out, there has to be a payoff. I spearheaded a payoff for an injustice, and I believed I would be spiritually rewarded for it. The strength I felt certainly wasn't coming from me. God had touched me. So, for however many days the trial would last, in the end, it would pay off the cost of greed. It would pay off wickedness, somehow. *I can do all things through Christ who strengthens me. I can do all things through Christ who strengthens me. I can do all things—*

The courtroom felt warm and inviting, rather than cold and distant. Maybe that was a good omen. Then, Isabelle Montague and her daughter Marjorie Davenport marched in. They took seats near us, and nervous excitement filled the air. Drake sauntered in and took a seat at the defense table next to his attorney. Maybe today he would break loose and tell the truth, and free himself from the prison of lies he had built. I hoped he would. I prayed that he would. I prayed that our family could forgive and move forward, reunite and be made whole once again.

The judge took the bench. The bailiff ordered all cell phones and electronic devices to be silenced. The bailiff announced, "Please stand. The court of Judge Adelle Pinkstrom is called to order."

The pleasant, grandmotherly looking judge mounted the bench.

"You may all be seated," the bailiff said.

The clerk handed Judge Pinkstrom a calendar, which she quickly perused. After a few short cases, the bailiff called us.

"The court calls the case of Drake Black vs. Danielle Carrington."

"Have both parties had the benefit of a mediation session and genuinely tried to settle this case?" Judge Pinkstrom asked.

"Yes," Elliott Spillinger, my attorney, said.

"Yes," Ora Mae Duffy, Drake's attorney, said.

"And I take it you were not able to work things out," the judge said.

"Right," Attorney Spillinger said.

"That's right," Ora Mae Duffy added.

When the judge mentioned the mediation hearing, I remembered it as if it were yesterday. Spencer, Isabelle Montague, Marjorie Davenport, my attorney, and I were there. Drake and his attorney, Ora Mae Duffy, were also present. I felt the session was both a waste of money and a waste of precious time. Yes, each side had to split the cost of $1,000 for the mediator's fee, which had to be paid before the mediation could take place. Both sides paid for the circus to begin.

Each side had been secluded from the other. I couldn't wait to hear Drake's proposal. I thought the very nature of mediation was to try to get both sides of the issue to come to the center, as much as possible. I also thought it meant that both sides would bring something to the table, something to offer as a concession. Drake had nothing of value to bring, not even the truth.

It was good that the parties were in different rooms because, after the mediator went back and forth for approximately 30 to 45 minutes, it was concluded that this mediation hearing would do nothing to resolve the matter at hand. There was nothing left. Drake had taken all the money. The only thing that remained was the house. Yes, the house belonging to Isabelle Montague and her granddaughter, Rachel. Before we actually said "no way" to the mediator's last you've-got-to-be-kidding demand from Drake, we said we would consider what he wanted if he made it clear what he wanted. He sent the mediator to us with his proposal.

"I'll cease my demands if you give me a thirty-eight thousand interest in the house."

Oh, my, he didn't say that, did he? Be still, my heart! What planet did Drake come from? He had no shame! We sent the mediator back to him with, "No way!" I wrote, "No, that's not up for consideration."

The mediator looked embarrassed as he turned and walked toward the office where Drake was waiting.

* * *

The judge's voice interrupted my memories of the mediation. "Are you ready to proceed?"

"Yes," Drake's attorney said.

My attorney, Elliott Spillinger, said, "Yes."

"Your Honor, we would ask that Isabelle Montague wait outside until she is called?" Attorney Duffy said.

"Why?" the judge asked.

"Because she is a witness in this case," Attorney Duffy said.

Why would Drake do that to Isabelle? Allowing her to remain in the courtroom wouldn't hurt one soul.

Isabelle gathered her things and, with assistance from her daughter Marjorie and my husband Spencer, left the courtroom. She made her way through the huge double doors into the lonely hallway.

"Let's continue," the judge said. "The court calls Drake Black to the witness stand."

Drake strolled to the witness stand. Marjorie, Spencer, and I eyed him. He didn't cast us even a glance as he passed.

"Raise your right hand," the bailiff said.

Drake raised his right hand.

"Do you swear to tell the truth, the whole truth, and nothing but the truth, so help you God?"

"I do," Drake swore.

Drake was on the witness stand, testifying with his eyes closed. What was up with that? I guess it was too hard for him to keep his lies straight if he kept his eyes open. Or, maybe it was because I was in the direct path of his vision. If he had opened his eyes, he would have been looking right at me, and that, perhaps, would be more than he could stand.

Drake swore again to tell the truth. The question was, whether he even knew what the truth was. Was this day going to be any different from all the others? Would today be the breakthrough day for him?

Elliott Spillinger began. "Before June 25, 2004, where did you live?"

"2401 Watley Avenue, Coral Springs, California," Drake said.

"Who owns the house?"

"Lawrence Black, my father," Drake said.

"How old are you?"

"Fifty-nine."

"Were you working in June two-thousand four?" Attorney Spillinger asked.

"No."

"Did you have a job in June two-thousand four?"

"No."

"Between June 2004 and December 2004, did you have a job?"

"No."

"What source of income did you have between June 2004 and December 2004?"

"U.S. Marine Corp's retirement of eleven hundred a month."

"What rank did you retire at?"

"Sergeant First Class."

"Any other income besides the Marine's retirement?"

"My aunt paid me six hundred and fifty a month."

"Any other income?"

"That's it."

"You moved in June 25, 2004?"

"Yes."

"When did you move out?" Attorney Spillinger asked.

"December 2004," Drake barked.

"You left the premises in December 2004?"

"No."

"What day?"

"November 30."

"From June 2004, did you take care of Lucille Stanton by yourself?"

"Yes."

"Was anyone else living with you?"

"No."

"Did anyone help you?"

"Juniper Black."

"How often did Juniper Black come over?"

"As needed."

"When did she start coming?"

"She started coming the latter part of August, September."

"How many days per week did she come?" Attorney Spillinger asked.

"Two to three times a week."

"Same for August, September, October?"

"Yes."

"Would she help you with Lucille Stanton?"

"Yes."

"During this period, did you give Lucille Stanton any sleeping pills?" Attorney Spillinger asked.

"Yes."

"When did it begin?"

"Didn't keep count."

"Why did you give her sleeping pills?"

"She had problems relaxing."

"So, in a thirty-day period, you gave her one or two a week?

"Yes."

"Did you ever read the label?"

"No."

"Did she ask you for the pills or did she take them herself?"

"I gave her the pills."

"From June to October, did you ever get her prescriptions refilled?"

"No."

"Did you ever run out of sleeping pills?"

"May have in July and August."

"After you ran out, did she take any other pills?"

"No."

"Did you know that she kept money in a shoe box?"

"No"

"Did you accompany her to Bank of America and go into the safe deposit box?"

"Yes."

"Why?"

"Because she wanted to take her money out," he said huffily.

"Did she trust you?"

"With all her heart, body, and soul."

"Were you in the room?"

"Yes."

"You didn't look to see what was in the safe deposit box?"

"No."

"Did she empty the box herself?"

"Yes."

"Did she have arthritis?"

"Yes."

"Did she have rheumatoid arthritis?"

"I don't know."

"Did you ever ask the doctor about her condition?"

"No."

"Why not?"

"Just didn't."

"Did you care about her?"

"Yes."

"So, she emptied the box. What did she do with the contents in the box?"

"She took it home to her house."

"What did she do with the contents?"

"Put it in her purse."

"Then where did you go?"

"Went to the DMV in Long Beach to get an I.D. card. Went to lunch at Red Lions and then went home."

"Did she empty the contents of her purse at home?"

"Don't know, never saw, and don't know where the contents of the box is."

"When did she talk to you about the contents of the box?"

"She came to me, talked to me, and gave me the contents."

"What was in the box?"

"Don't recall."

"What else did she give you?"

"Told me to take care of her money."

"Was it fifty, sixty, or seventy thousand dollars?"

"Ten thousand."

"What did you do with it?"

"Kept it."

The gasp in the courtroom didn't seem to bother Drake's conscience one bit. He smirked and leaned back. Judge Pinkstrom called a well-deserved recess. Everyone moved quickly out of the courtroom and emptied into the halls, giving an opinion about Drake taking his aunt's money. Though I was too happy to get out of the courtroom, I couldn't wait to hear the rest after recess. Those were questions that just might make Drake think twice about what he had done. Otherwise, I don't think he would ever have thought he did anything wrong.

Chapter 33

Almost before I had time to use the bathroom and wash my hands with the liquid pine-smelling soap, it was time to return to the courtroom. When I got back, the others were already there, and Drake was already on the witness stand. My attorney was pumping him with questions.

"Did you know Elroy Bell in June 2004?"

"No."

"When did you meet him?"

"Met him in July 2004."

"Did you meet his wife?"

"Yes."

"Have you done any business with Mr. Bell, like real estate or proposed real estate transactions?"

"No."

"Did Lucille Stanton ever say anything about her neighbors?"

"She said they were the best neighbors she ever had."

"Did you ask her why?"

"No."

"Did Lucille Stanton ever tell you she had a trust?"

"No."

"When did you first learn about the 2000 trust?"

"October 19, 2004."

"When did you first learn about the 2004?"

"I was asked to come to the Bell's house and witness the signing."

"Who asked you?"

"Lucille Stanton."

"When did she ask you? The a.m. or p.m.?"

"She said we were going to the Bells because she 'got something for me.'"

"Any more conversation?"

"No."

"How did she get to the Bells?"

"She walked."

"Why didn't you go with her?"

"I was straightening the house."

"How much time passed before you went to the Bells?"

"Five minutes."

"Who was there?"

"The Bells, Desquita Raunche, Lettie Dolson."

"What happened from the time you walked in until the time you left?"

"We sat at the dining room table and Elroy said he'd read the will."

"What else happened?"

"The reading was confirmed by Lucille Stanton and we left."

"How much time elapsed?"

"Between a half-hour and forty-five minutes."

"Mr. Black, I would ask that you look at Exhibit Y, the copy of a check," Attorney Spillinger said. "Do you recognize it?"

"Yes."

"When did you see it?"

"October first, two-thousand four."

"The check is made payable to **Dillard Business Works.** Was the check made out while you were at the dining room table? Did you ask what name was to go on the check?"

"No."

"Who entered the seven hundred fifty dollars?"

"Bell said it was the price of the trust."

"Who prepared the trust?"

"Elroy Bell."

The judge maintained a poker face. But Drake Black's answers were so preposterous. Judge Pinkstrom rolled her eyes to the ceiling, as if to say, I don't believe what I'm hearing. She interrupted the questioning and cast her eyes at Drake.

"What is Mr. Bell's line of work?"

"I don't know."

"You live by him and you don't know what he does?"

"Roofer."

"What does your neighbor do for a living?"

"Roofer."

"The check was not written to a roofing company. What kind of business is Dillard Business Works?"

"Ma'am, I don't know."

"You said the payee was put in after Lucille Stanton had left the location. Was the payee left blank?" the judge persisted.

"Yes."

"Was he a laywer? You left the line blank."

"I don't know."

Attorney Spillinger resumed his questioning. "This check was written from the account of the Lucille Stanton Living Trust. Did that indicate to you that a living trust was already in existence?"

"Yes."

"Did you ask what the check was for?"

"Never wrote a check."

"Did you write a check on this account?"

"No."

"Did you ever write a check on this account?"

"No."

"Did you ask Lucille Stanton who prepared the 2004 trust?"

"I didn't ask her."

"Did you ask Mr. Bell if he prepared the trust?"

"No, I had no idea who prepared the trust."

"Who wrote out the trust, I mean who wrote out the words on paper?" Attorney Spillinger asked.

"I guess my auntie did."

"Who recorded the document?"

"I did. I took it to Norwalk."

"When?"

"October first."

"How come?"

"It was a document being processed that day."

"Was it a rush?"

"No rush, just a good day."

"Did you want the document recorded, or did your aunt?"

"My aunt wanted it."

"Who wrote out the words?"

"I don't know."

"As you sit here today, you don't know who drafted this document?"

"No."

"Did you read Elroy Bell's deposition?"

"No."

"Did you ever ask who drafted this document?"

"No."

"Was there any conversation about who Lucille Stanton was leaving her house to?"

"She said she was leaving it to me."

"Somewhere around September twenty through twenty-eight, was there something happening that might have changed her mind from leaving the house to the nieces and nephews to making you sole heir?"

"No. I was just jubilant that she thought that much of me."

"What was the conversation with Lucille on September twenty?" Attorney Spillinger asked.

"Drake, you the only one that did anything for me. I asked you to come and live with me and you did."

"In June two-thousand four, were you speaking with anyone in the family?"

"I spoke with my mother, my sisters, my brother."

"Did you know that Lucille Stanton decided to leave her house to Isabelle and Rachel?"

"No."

"Would you be surprised that everyone else knew?"

"Yes."

"Did Lucille Stanton ask you to file any papers in September 2004?" Attorney Spillinger said. "Now turn to page two. On the first page it says plaintiff Lucille Stanton—"

"Did she—"

Judge Pinkstrom's eyes rolled up again. She interrupted the questioning again and asked, "Mr. Black, is this your handwriting? Page two, paragraph nine?"

"Yes."

"Did Lucille Stanton dictate this to you?"

"Yes."

"Word for word?"

"Yes."

"Is this her signature on the last page? Did Lucille Stanton sign her signature?" Judge Pinkstrom asked.

"Yes."

"She signed it?"

"Correct."

"Did you plan to get a conservatorship after the restraining order hearing?" the judge asked.

"Yes."

"Refer to Exhibit AA," the judge continued. "Why did you want a conservatorship?"

"So my auntie could live out her last days in her own home."

"Was it drafted?"

"Elroy Bell started that."

"Who did you tell?"

"I was given instructions by the court."

Attorney Spillinger resumed his questioning. "Did you know what you had to show to get a conservatorship? What condition the person needed to be in? Did anyone tell you that?"

"No."

"Did your aunt have help to walk?"

"No, she had a cane, walker, a wheelchair."

"How many times did you take your aunt to the doctor?"

"Two."

"And how many times did Juniper take her?"

"One."

"Anyone else?"

"No."

"Did you ask the doctor how she was; what was going on with her?"

"No."

"Did you know she had hearing aids?"

"Yes."

"Did she wear them?"

"No."

"What's your first wife's name?"

"Eunice."

"After September 2005, did you give her ten thousand dollars?"

"No, sir."

"Did she give you a cashier's check after September 2004?"

"No."

"Did you travel in 2004?"

"Yes."

"Where did you go?"

"To Kentucky, Maryland, and Las Vegas."

"How long did you stay?"

"Two weeks."

"Did you take your ex-wife?"

"Yes."

"Who else?"

"My grand-boys."

"Did you travel in 2004?"

"No."

"2006?"

No."

"You moved out November thirty, 2004?"

"Yes."

"But you moved back in December 2005. Why?"

"It was my house. I never should have left."

Attorney Spillinger showed Drake Exhibit CC, a copy of the contents of Lucille Stanton's house.

"Do you recognize any of the items on this list?"

"Yes. Danielle Carrington gave away most everything in the house, furniture, TVs. She even gave away some of my things."

The Judge stopped Drake. "Where is the car?"

"In the garage."

"Who's driving it?"

"It's undriveable."

"Who has the pink slip?"

"I have it."

"You get Lucille Stanton's house. Nobody else gets anything?"

The judge directed a question to me. "Mrs. Carrington, can you bring me a copy of your family tree tomorrow?"

"Yes," I answered.

The judge continued to question Drake. "Did you know you had a duty to report any money in those accounts to the court?"

"No."

"Did you give an account to the court?"

"No."

"Did she ever ask where her money was?"

"Yes."

"What did she say?"

"Drake, where did you put my money?"

"And what was your response?" Attorney Spillinger asked.

"I told her I put it in the closet."

Judge Pinkstrom interrupted. "Where did you put it in the closet?"

"In the linen and utility-type closet."

"How much money was there?"

"Around ten thousand."

"That was your money. Why did you put it in the closet?"

"It was a good place."

"Why not in the bank?"

"Bank?"

"So, why didn't you open up an account? Did you put it in your bank? How much money was there? What did you do with that money?" the judge asked.

"Put it in the checking account."

"What checking account?"

"My account."

"Is there another bunch of money?"

"No."

"So, it went from the bank to your aunt's house?"

"Yes."

Attorney Spillinger showed the Police Report Exhibit to Drake. "If you will refer to page two."

"The police asked about the seventy-thousand dollars when they interviewed you. Did you tell the police it was seventy thousand dollars?" Attorney Spillinger asked.

"I didn't tell them seventy thousand dollars. I told them ten thousand dollars."

"At the October 2004 hearing, did you give oral testimony that there was three thousand in the box?"

"I said a few thousand dollars."

"Now, you're saying it was ten thousand dollars?"

"I didn't make any accounting."

"During the time you lived with Lucille Stanton, did you know the names of her doctors?"

"I only remember Price."

"Did you know she had weakness, hypertension, muscle fiber weakness? Did you know she had any of these conditions?"

"Only thing I knew was arthritis and hypertension."

"Rheumatoid?"

"I don't know."

"Was she using a walker?"

"Yes."

Attorney Spillinger showed Drake Exhibit W Medical Order Form, where he received a call regarding a bathroom potty for the bedroom.

"Why did she need this? How far was the bathroom from the bedroom?" Attorney Spillinger asked.

"Not that far, but for comfort."

"How far is her door to the bathroom? Is it farther than the Bell's house?"

"No."

"Why did she need a wheel chair?" Attorney Spillinger asked.

"For mobility. So she could get around."

"I don't know what you mean."

"We had to walk to the front door from the courtroom to the front door."

"On October first, two-thousand four, when she walked to the Bells, did she walk alone?"

"Yes."

"No further questions, your honor," Attorney Spillinger said.

Drake stalked from the witness stand and sat at the defense table. He sighed and slumped a bit.

Chapter 34

After what had happened in court that morning, the last place we wanted to be that afternoon was in Judge Pinkstrom's courtroom. But she ordered us back at 1:30, and so there we all sat.

Isabelle, her daughter Marjorie, Marjorie's husband Troy, her daughter Veronica, and Spencer and I took our familiar seats in front row center. My attorney told me after this morning's hearing that he was going to call me as a witness. At the time, I thought I would be okay with that, but after coming back from lunch, the thought of this whole fiasco got in my blood. It was going to be hard for me to restrain my emotions. I knew that because I was constantly having internal verbal battles with Drake. I didn't want to take a chance on having my pent-up emotions break loose on the witness stand.

At 1:30, Judge Pinkstrom signaled the court clerk to have everyone re-enter the courtroom. The courtroom bailiff stood and announced, "Please turn off all cell phones and electronic equipment."

The court clerk announced, "All rise."

"Thank you, ladies and gentleman. We are back in court in the matter of Drake Black vs. Danielle Carrington. Mr. Spillinger, I understand you will be calling the first witness."

"Yes, Your Honor. I call Danielle Carrington."

I made slow but deliberate steps to the witness stand, my stomach fluttering like butterflies in a jar.

"Mrs. Carrington, please raise your right hand. Do you swear to tell the truth, the whole truth, and nothing but the truth, so help you God?" the clerk asked.

"I do. I do. I do."

"Did you know Lucille Stanton?"

"Yes."

"Who was she?"

"She was my father's oldest sister."

"Do you know where she lived?"

"Yes."

"Do you know the address of her house?"

"Yes. Eighty-five ten Menlo Avenue, Los Angeles."

"Do you know how long she lived at this address?"

"Fifty-two years."

"When did you begin helping Lucille Stanton?"

"I began helping her in October of ninety-six, after her husband died."

"Where do you live?"

"Nine zero one Maplewood Road, Redondo Beach."

"How far is your house from Ms. Stanton's?"

"Approximately eleven miles."

"How often would you go to visit Lucille Stanton?"

"One to two times per week."

"Did you take Ms. Stanton to her doctor appointments?"

"Yes, before Drake Black moved in."

"Where is her doctor's office located?"

"At the Brighton Clinic in Copley."

"Besides taking Lucille Stanton to the doctor, what other things did you do for her?"

"I did things for her like taking her shopping to buy clothes, out to lunch...."

"Mrs. Carrington, let's go back to the question regarding Lucille Stanton's doctor appointments. After the appointment, what would you do?"

"Before I took her back home, we would go to a restaurant and eat. She loved doing that."

"In two thousand, did you take Lucille Stanton to see an attorney?"

"Yes."

"For what purpose?"

"She wanted to get a Living Trust."

"Was this her idea or yours?"

"I made the suggestion, and she agreed."

"Why did you suggest this to her?"

"I said to her that she needed to get one because if something happened to her, I didn't want to have any problems."

"Did you anticipate any problems?"

"Just wanted to be sure."

"Can you recall the name of the place where you took her to get the trust?"

"I think it was located in Downey."

"Do you have an address?"

"No, not at the moment. But I remember it was somewhere in Downey."

Judge Pinkstrom interrupted. "How many people stand to gain financial reward following Lucille Stanton's death?"

"A whole lot."

"Do you have a number?"

"Not exactly."

"Mrs. Carrington, tomorrow, I want you to bring me a copy of the family tree," the judge said.

"Okay."

Attorney Spillinger resumed his questioning. "Do you know anything about a missing safe deposit box key prior to September 21, 2004?"

"Yes."

"When was that?"

"In approximately May 2004, Lucille Stanton told me that her safe deposit box key was missing."

"And what did you do to assist Ms. Stanton with this?"

"I took her to the bank to get another box with a new key."

"Did you go in with her to see the new box?"

"Yes, I actually removed the property from the old box and put it in the new box."

"What was in the box?"

"Personal property like a marriage certificate, some personal receipts, the pink slip for a car she owned, and money."

"Did you count the money?"

"No."

"How thick were the stacks?"

"Oh, about 2 inches thick."

"Do you know what the denominations were?"

"They were all fifties and hundreds."

"Did Lucille Stanton have arthritis?"

"Yes."

"For how long?"

"For years. She had a total knee replacement, I think, in 1995."

"Do you know of any other medical problems Lucille Stanton had?"

"She complained of dizziness."

"When?"

"In 2002 and 2003."

"Did she go to the doctor?"

"Yes."

"And what he did do?"

"He prescribed medication."

"Do you recall an incident regarding the bathtub?"

"Yes."

"What happened?"

"I received a call from a cousin saying she had not spoken with Lucille for two days."

"Was that unusual?"

"Yes, because my cousin spoke with Lucille Stanton every night before going to bed."

"And what did you do?"

"My husband Spencer and my son Travis went with me to see about her."

"What did you discover?"

"She had slipped in the bathtub and couldn't get out."

"How long had she been in the tub?"

"For almost three days."

"Were the paramedics called?"

"Yes."

"Who called the paramedics?"

"I believe I did."

"When they came, what did they do?"

"They stabilized her and took her to the hospital."

"Did you go to the hospital with her?"

"Both my husband and I went to the hospital with her."

"Then what happened?"

"They decided to admit her to the hospital."

"How long did she stay in the hospital?"

"For five days."

"Then what happened?"

"She was sent to a rehab center."

"Did Lucille Stanton file a restraining order against you?"

"Well, according to court papers, she did."

"When you went to court on October 19, 2004, what happened?"

"Lucille Stanton was sent home with me."

"When you went back to Lucille Stanton's house on that night, did Drake Black say anything to you?"

"Yes."

"What did he say?"

I automatically became animated. I know it wasn't the best thing to do, but my nerves were raw. I answered Mr. Spillinger using every inflection in my voice I could think of. I even changed my voice to mimic Drake. I wanted the scene in court to accurately reflect what had gone on at Lucille's house when we returned that night.

If looks could kill! Mr. Spillinger's look told me I had crossed the line. But I was okay with that because the full flavor of what had happened that night was unleashed. After my display of raw emotions, Mr. Spillinger tried hard to gather himself and continued questioning me.

"Then what happened?"

"I told Drake in a most emphatic tone that Aunt Lucille was not going to stay with him."

The judge interrupted Mr. Spillinger's questioning.

"Mr. Spillinger, we will take a recess until tomorrow morning at eight thirty."

"Thank you, Your Honor," Mr. Spillinger stated.

"Mrs. Carrington, you may step down."

We all left the courtroom and briefly stopped in the hallway. Mr. Spillinger blasted me for the outburst where I mimicked Drake. I told him I understood the reason he was upset, and I did. Did I regret doing it? I didn't. The court needed the benefit of the harassment I had gone through that night, and a hundred nights before. Now everyone knew exactly what happened that night, and I felt better.

Chapter 35

June 7, 2006: Dear God. This is the second day of this trial, and I feel like I've lost a year that I might have used helping the sick, reading to old people, and/or increasing my business. Danielle kept writing from the floral chair in the living room near her bed.

My husband and I started a wholesale business from scratch seven years ago, and it blossomed with our discipline of going to work on time, giving our clients professional attention, and providing excellent customer service. Now it had begun to look like a neglected apple orchard. Seeking justice, though, was the one thing that drove me. I had no other choice, even while attorneys gobbled up nearly a hundred thousand dollars in fees and there was little time to seek new contracts to replenish what we were spending.

I would have to wait until every testimony was given and the judge had spoken the final word. I wasn't quite sure what to expect, but I was sure that my head would go from side to side watching the side shows. If the testimony of Drake's witnesses remotely resembled their deposition testimonies, we were all in for a bumpy ride!

The courtroom was quiet and somber. I eased into the front seat. My husband Spencer made a detour, but found his way into the courtroom. He had been through every bit of the travesty with me. I still recall him saying it was fine with him for Lucille to come and live with us. He never questioned the decision. I felt that bond of understanding that very moment.

How I wanted the process to be over! Maybe today the judge would make her final ruling. Court began with Elroy Bell testifying. If his testimony was anywhere as dramatic as his deposition, this case should be one for the books!

While Drake sat at the defense table with his attorney, the court called Elroy Bell to the

witness stand. The clerk swore him in.

"Mr. Bell, do you promise to tell the truth, the whole truth, and nothing but the truth, so help you God?"

"I do," Elroy Bell said.

* * *

I recalled April 12, 2006, when Elroy Bell was on the hot seat at the deposition. My attorney, Elliott Spillinger, had given Elroy a list of things to bring to the deposition. Elroy made excuses for not bringing them. He even seemed agitated, as if the request had been meaningless and the conversation unimportant. Attorney Spillinger rose from his seat, staring at the papers in his hand. He didn't crack a smile.

"We'll be working from Exhibit 1. You can compare your documents with mine and see if they're the same ones I want to work off. The court reporter will be attaching them to the booklet."

"Right," Elroy said.

"Mr. Bell, could you take a look at the documents that are described?"

"Uh-huh."

"All writings that refer on their face to the Lucille Stanton Living Trust dated October 12, 2000," Attorney Spillinger said. "Were you able to find any of those documents and bring them here today?"

"The only documents that I have are relevant to the trust that was drafted to assist Lucille." Elroy Bell shifted on the brown sofa, and his feet twisted outward on the multigrain-colored carpet. Elroy continued. "I think one thing should be brought up in advance here. Many of the materials were prepared on a computer. Unfortunately, while working, someone came into the office, stole a lot of the computers, and one of them was the computer that had Lucille's materials in it."

"Okay."

"I do have a copy of a police report. It's missing at this time, but I'm sure it's on record with the police department, though."

"And how many different computers was Lucille's information on?"

"One."

"And was that in your house?"

"No."

"Where was it?"

"At the company. At the time that company would be Granville Roofing Company."

"So, Lucille's information was on the computer at the Granville Roofing Company?"

"Yes."

"And that computer was stolen?"

"Yes. Along with several others, yes."

"About when was that?"

"End of 2004."

"Okay."

"However, I was able to – in regards to your subpoena, I did have a file that provided a copy of the check that was paid to me. A copy of the hard draft of the trust that was made for Lucille's declarations. There was a declaration of Drake Black that had never, I guess, been filed. A copy of the living trust that Lucille had provided to me and dated October 12, 2000."

Elroy fumbled through his tattered, disorganized briefcase. "Well, well, this here is a copy of the book I used to prepare her trust—"How to Avoid Probate by Creating a Living Trust." He looked up with an unintelligible smirk.

"Well, let me just see what you just described."

"Go ahead and take that."

"This is the October 12 trust. And I can't remember the one you just handed over, was that the 2000?"

"That's the one for 2000, which is Number 1 that you had."

"Okay. Fine. The next item is Number 2. This is the 2004 trust."

"That's in there also."

"The one—"

"Uh-huh."

"Okay. And all that stuff looks like correspondence concerning the 2000 trust. Do you have anything that—"

"There was no correspondence in writing concerning the 2000 trust."

"Okay. I guess you're saying there's no written correspondence with anyone?"

"Right."

"You don't have any correspondence pertaining to Danielle Carrington?"

"I believe the only written materials that may exist would be in the hands of the LAPD. And that may be relevant, I don't know. And that would be the document. I mean that would be a phone call where I call 911."

"Any documents that constitute bank records regarding Lucille?"

"The only bank records that are known to me would be what's on the trust, the actual trust that I provided to you. It provides a bank account number."

"Receipts from the sale of any property owned by Lucille Stanton?"

"I would not have any knowledge of any receipts for the sale of property of Lucille Stanton."

I shook my head at the audacity of such bold-faced lies. Attorney Spillinger wiped his brow, glanced at his watch, and stood. I could see we were going to get a lunch break. I could sure use a break. Elroy sighed as if he had just gotten out of a pot of boiling water!

* * *

I dreaded coming back into that office. I felt the urge to run away. The gray walls seemed to be walking toward me from each side. And just to look at Elroy, his big eyes shifting from side to side, made me want to puke. I took my seat, fully engaged in this circus!

Attorney Spillinger began. "Do you have anything for number ten?"

Elroy shook his head.

"You have nothing in writing at all, Mr. Bell? How about number eleven?"

"Again, there may be writings which are notes. Those might have been inside of that computer," Elroy said.

"Right."

"Now keep in mind, oftentimes people use what is called a floppy, but because Granville Roofing closed down, a lot of things were in storage. You know, there may be something in writing, but as far as locating the floppy, we were unable to locate it," Elroy attempted to explain.

"When did Granville close down"?

"Granville closed down, oh, October of last year."

"Okay. So when was the theft?"

"The theft was in, right after –that was in 2004, the theft."

"Number fifteen."

"Again, the only other writings I believe may be available would be the notary, a part of exhibit, the trust. This is not the copy of the original. The original is filed with the Los Angeles County Recorder's Office, which would have the individual seal of that individual who notarized everything."

"Well, the original is mailed. It's mailed back to someone. Did you receive the original?"

"No."

"Do you know who did?"

"No."

"Number twenty-two."

"All writings that show Lucille was of sound mind? I don't quite understand that one."

"Okay. Number twenty-five."

"All writings that show Lucille did not suffer from memory loss. I'm not a medical expert. I don't know who Lucille saw, if she had a memory loss or anything. So, I couldn't answer that at all."

"Okay. Number twenty-seven."

"All writings that show Lucille was not infirm."

"You don't have any records on her medications?"

"All records that constitute records of medications taken by Lucille. No."

"Can you tell me your occupational history briefly?"

"I have no occupational history."

"Okay. What's your occupation now?"

"I'm unemployed."

"And how long have you been unemployed?"

"I'm on disability, but I don't receive monies from disability. I was the administrator of an estate, but that doesn't make me employed for the last five, six years. Yeah, for the last six years I've been the administrator of an estate."

"So before you became—"

"I should also say now that I've worked in assisting various attorneys."

"We'll get to that. Where else were you employed?"

"Fable Helps."

"Is that a DBA?"

"Yes."

"When did you walk away from that business?"

"2000 to. Let's see, 2005. How do I describe it?"

"Just the year is fine."

"I mean, I've really not even walked away from it."

"Okay."

"I have a few attorney friends. When they have problems on certain issues or anything, they'll call me. I assist them with paperwork under the name of Fable Helps."

"What are the attorneys' names?"

"John Anton is one of them. I used to do work for Edward Barrett. He's messed up now."

"Edward who?"

"Edward Barrett."

"Okay. Anyone else?"

"I've done a lot of things in pro per for people. I've been recognized by the California State Supreme Court."

"Recognized in what respect?"

"Filing a writing, writ of mandamus, having issues with the courts that I had reversed in pro per."

"How long have you known Drake Black?"

"I met Drake in 2004."

"When in 2004?"

"I'm bad with dates. So—"

"Just do your best."

* * *

The judge checked her watch, and, like magic, we walked out of the heat of that room for a break. I ate the tasteless burger like a robot in the cafeteria, while hoping I never had to go back in that courtroom. I was wasting my time on a crazy man. A crazy man's lies were going to affect my aunt's living trust. They were going to affect her last wishes. The culmination of a person's life was being affected by a lying neighbor, a crazy man. I had to live and see it through.

Chapter 36

Yes, we had to return to court and stay there until the heavy traffic hour of 4 o'clock. The judge jumped right into getting the show on the road. After the opening, Attorney Spillinger had gotten his second wind. He asked Elroy Bell his first question.

"When did you first meet Mr. Black? 2004?"

"Yes."

"And what were the, the circumstances that you met him? Just walking on the street, or—"

"No. Lucille is my neighbor, my next-door neighbor. So I would see Lucille during the mornings and we would talk. And she actually introduced me to Drake and informed me that he was her nephew."

"Okay. Was he living in her house at that time?"

"No. You're asking me somewhat of a vague question when you say was he living in that house at that time. Because when she introduced Drake as her nephew, he was–at least I perceived him as someone that was staying there watching over her. I would say, at that point, but yes, he began to reside there."

"So you're telling me that your house is immediately next door to hers on the same side of the street?"

"Yes."

"Okay. So, from the time you first met Mr. Black until today, have you socialized with him?"

"I've spoken to him, yes."

"Okay. And what is the nature of that socializing?"

"In passing. Things like, 'Hey, how's it going? What's going on with you?' General conversation. Nothing to make us, more or less, associates."

"Okay. Have you had any business dealings with Mr. Black since you first met him?"

"No."

"You're familiar with what I've marked as Exhibit two, the 2000 trust?"

"Yes."

"When did you first see it?"

"When Lucille provided it to me."

"And when was that?"

"Oh, God. I would say that it was in September, I believe it would be."

"Of?"

"Two-thousand four. Yeah, September 2004."

"And where was she when she gave it to you?"

"In her yard."

"Okay. And what did she do? She called you on the phone, or –"

"No. Every morning, Lucille would get up and come out in her yard."

"So you were outside at the same time she was?"

"Uh-huh. I've talked to Lucille – my relationship with Lucille went way back before then. Our relationship went back to 2002."

"But let me just try and focus on this. The time when she gave you the trust, she was in the backyard?"

"No. Front yard."

"And she called you over? How—"

"Me and Lucille had been talking. I believe it was in early September. And she kept saying to me she was having a problem with her niece. She was very upset and said her niece was Danielle Carrington. I think it may have been a week or two later when she was outside, and she said, 'Elroy, I need to talk to you. I found the paperwork I've been looking for.' And she provided me with this document and she told me that she needed to do something about it."

"Okay. And what else did she say?"

"I says, 'Okay. What is it?'"

"She said that no one was helping her except for her nephew, Drake. And since no one was helping her, she wanted to make sure that no one got anything but Drake. And there are witnesses to that, too."

"Well, who are the witnesses?"

"Well, later –"

"Slow down. Let's just focus in on this conversation you had with Lucille in the yard."

"Well, there were several conversations."

"Let's just take that one. Tell me all you remember about that conversation when she first raised the subject of the trust?"

"I just can't recall it at this time."

"Was there anyone else present?"

"Just me and Lucille. Oh, yeah. There was someone that was present. I'm confusing two different times now. The second time–"

"We're still on the first time?"

"No."

"No witnesses?"

"No."

"Let's go to the next time you talked to Lucille about the subject of this trust. When was that–the next day, the next week, what?"

"Maybe a couple of weeks later. I informed her that we were working on everything and that as a result of working on things, she would have to come over and sign things. Of course, she didn't like taking drives, so we arranged for the notary. I informed her that a notary would come to the house, my house. And she says, 'Okay, fine. Just let me know when you finish.' She kept asking me how much I was going to charge her to do things. I said I had to pick up materials to determine how much it's worth," Elroy stated.

"When was the next conversation?"

"When all of us were sitting at the table together. I went and got Lucille. I also went and got Drake because I wanted him to make sure he signed documents with the notary present also."

"Tell me about the conversations in your house."

"The persons that were present at my house again was the notary, my wife, myself, of course Lucille, and then Drake. Oh, and Desquita Raunche was there also."

"Who is Desquita Raunche?"

"Desquita, she's–at the time she was acting in the position of doing secretarial work for me."

"Is she related to you?"

"No."

"Does she still do secretarial work?"

"I would say that she does, yes."

"So tell me the conversations that went on. At your table–what day was that?"

"October, it would be October 1, 2004."

"And how long was everybody at the–at your table in your house?"

"Maybe an hour, half-hour to an hour."

"Tell me what was said."

"Well, at that time I sat down and I read everything word for word inside of this trust, Exhibit four and Exhibit three, to Lucille. Prior to reading this, she made it clear that the reason she was doing this is because she wanted to make sure that Drake got her home. She wanted to make sure that Danielle Carrington did not get anything. This is what she said at the table. She had an issue with Danielle because Danielle kept trying to put her in a convalescent home."

"And where did you get the notary's number?"

"Where did I get the notary's number?"

"Did you know the notary?"

"No."

"Where did you get her –"

"I believe my wife called around until she was able to locate a notary."

"Right. Okay. After October first, two-thousand four, did you speak to Lucille again concerning the trust?"

"After that did I speak with Lucille again concerning the trust?"

"Correct."

"I would say, yes, I did."

"How many times?"

"Oh, my goodness. After the trust, I saw Lucille–"

"Before you do that, how many times?"

"I can't quite say how many times I saw Lucille."

"More than two?"

"Of course more than two times."

"More than five?"

"More than five. She's my neighbor."

"You're talking about the trust now, as opposed to cutting the grass or barbecuing?"

"How many times did we talk about the trust?" Elroy repeated the question.

"At all? None or two or three?"

"After October first, she would look at me. She would smile. She would always say, 'Thank you. Thank you for helping me.' I made sure that Lucille had all of her documents in order and she kept them. She kept her documents."

"Did you talk about the trust?"

"Yes. Yes."

"How many times?"

"Her only concern was to make sure everything went to Drake, and I would say that conversation may have occurred only one other time, not two, three or four or five times."

"When would that be?"

"That would be right after October first. You know, I don't know if this here assists us or helps in any way, but you got to understand, Lucille was there and she was becoming frail until this guy stepped in, her nephew, and she became healthy. Her appearance changed. Everything about her changed for the better, for the good. She deteriorated later."

"You said that Lucille gave you this when?" Attorney Spillinger handed Elroy the number two living trust.

"This would be in September that she gave this document to me."

"Okay. So did you give this to her on October first?" Mr. Spillinger asked.

"She may have received her copy that was unrecorded."

"Okay. Well, let me—"

"What's your back date, so I can keep fresh with my dates here?"

"I'm going to mark that now. Because you didn't have that one."

"The back page. Because, again, this was my hard notes." Elroy attempted to explain.

"Here's what I've marked as Exhibit 10. Take a look at that."

"This is the same day that she received first a copy of the one that was unrecorded and then it was taken and recorded that day and she, I believe, received the recorded copy then," Elroy Bell stated.

"Well, here's my question. I'm going to put in front of you Exhibit three and Exhibit ten. You'll notice that Exhibit three says September 28, 2004."

"Right."

"Exhibit ten says October 1, 2004. I'm not going to go through the text. I don't know if there are changes or not. My question is simple. Is there some reason why this one is dated September 28, 2004, and this one is dated October 1, 2004?" Mr. Spillinger inquired.

"Yes, there is."

"Please."

"When you requested me to produce documents, you requested hard documents. This was the drafts of everything, okay. And this document here would be considered the draft."

"By this, you mean 3?"

"Exhibit 3 and 4 is just a draft."

"When was that draft prepared?"

"In September."

"How about the date?"

"Oh, God. That would be in my notes in the computer. But the best I can give you would be September."

"My question is, after you finished it, did you show it to Lucille before October 1, 2004?" Mr. Spillinger asked.

"No."

"Okay. During the time you were preparing the 2004 trust, did you talk to Drake Black?"

"You mean in greeting him?"

"No. About the trust."

"No. That was not his business," Elroy Bell protested.

"I just want to take you back to the day that Lucille called you over when she was in the yard and said she wanted to talk to you about a problem, whatever you said. You remember that?"

"Uh-huh."

"Okay. Now, forward–let's go to October 1, 2004, when she came over to your house. How did she get over there?"

"She walked."

"And did everybody get there at the same time, or do you remember?"

"Roughly about the same time—eleven-thirty, because I informed everyone to be there at that time."

"And when did you inform everybody to be there, what day?"

"Maybe a day or two earlier previously."

Elroy began to twist in the chair. Sweat ran down his forehead, and he wiped it with his arm. Attorney Spillinger looked at him for almost a minute. "Thank you, Mr. Bell, for your time. You're free to leave."

That was the questioning that had brought us to this day, this hour. Wow, what a long mental escape. I was listening to Attorney Spillinger ask Elroy Bell pretty much the same questions he had asked him at the deposition hearing. Elroy Bell gave him the same lies, I mean answers. Ringling Brothers Circus had nothing on him from the witness stand. "Under oath" and "penalty of perjury" meant nothing to him.

"I have nothing else, your Honor," Mr. Spillinger said while turning to the judge.

"Mr. Bell, you may step down," Judge Pinkstrom said.

* * *

The court called Eunice Black to the witness stand. She made her way into the courtroom and to the witness stand.

"Raise your right hand. Do you promise to tell the truth, the whole truth, and nothing but the truth, so help you God?"

"I do."

"Do you know Lucille Stanton?" Attorney Spillinger asked.

"Yes."

"When did you meet her?"

"I met her once or twice in 1987 or '88."

"After you first met her, when was the next time you saw her?"

"2004, at my daughter's wedding, as I am Drake Black's first wife."

"Who do you live with?"

"My daughter and my son-in-law."

"On July 17, 2004, you went to Ms. Stanton's house?"

"Yes."

"For what reason?"

"Drake had made beef stew."

"Did you see Ms. Stanton?"

"Yes."

"Where was Ms. Stanton?"

"In her bedroom sitting on her bed."

"How long were you there?"

"Seven to ten minutes."

"In approximately 2004, Drake brought Lucille Stanton to your house; is that correct?"

"Yes."

"For what reason?"

"He brought her by for an outing."

"How did she appear?"

"She was alert and played with my two grandchildren."

"How long did they stay?"

"Ten to fifteen minutes."

"When they left your house, did Ms. Stanton walk out by herself?"

"Yes."

"She was not assisted at all?"

"No."

"She used no cane or a walker?"

"No. She walked by herself and got into the truck."

"In approximately April 2005, did you take a trip?"

"Yes."

"Did you go alone?"

"No."

"Who went with you?"

"Drake Black and my two grandchildren."

"Did Drake Black ever ask you to cash a check for ten thousand dollars?"

"No."

"Did Drake Black ever ask you to deposit ten thousand dollars into your checking account?"

"No."

"Your Honor, I have no further questions."

"Ms. Black, you may step down."

I guess Attorney Spillinger knew that the ex-wife was a part of the lies, or that she knew only what she knew and it didn't implicate her, so he cut her short. Everyone knew she was Drake's wife once, and that was that.

Chapter 37

We had managed to make our way back to the afternoon session. I had to fight my tiredness, my depression, and my thoughts of giving it all up. I just had to live for the possibility of hearing the judge rule in my favor. I knew that not one fair-minded person in the world would grant Drake entitlement to all of Lucille's worldly possessions. And even if some judge did grant Drake's greedy wish, and validate his bogus trust, it would do Drake no good. *The wealth of the wicked is heaped up for the righteous.* It's a spiritual law, I told myself.

At 2:30, we took our seats. It was already a pressure cooker in that courtroom. My mind found a way to escape the cooking of my brain, though. I thought of the crazy things that happened at the hearing yesterday. Drake closing his eyes to testify, his request for Isabelle to leave the courtroom, his wry smiles to the judge. I willed myself to stay awake, as tired as I was. Well, I had that private conversation, which I allowed to be just that.

My attorney told me that Dr. Walter Donoghue would be coming for the afternoon's hearing.

"I placed him on-call and haven't been able to reach him to let him know he'll be needed for sure," Attorney Spillinger said.

"We can only hope," I answered.

My eyes turned to those huge wooden doors, and I saw a gentleman with a slight hump in his back making his way into the courtroom. Dr. Donoghue!

Attorney Spillinger walked over to the doctor. I saw the two of them smiling and nodding. Yes, Dr. Donoghue had come.

Judge Pinkstrom took the bench, and the court was called to order.

"Ladies and gentleman, we are back in court in the case of Drake Black vs. Danielle Carrington."

"Mr. Spillinger, would you call your first witness?" Judge Pinkstrom asked.

"Dr. Walter Donoghue," Attorney Spillinger said.

Dr. Donoghue moved with a slightly awkward gait, and it took him a little longer than usual to reach the witness stand. He was sworn in quickly.

"Would you state your name for the record?" Attorney Spillinger asked.

"Walter Donoghue."

"Dr. Donoghue, what is your specialty?"

"Neurology."

"Who are you employed by?"

"Tinsdale Clinics."

"For how long?"

"For all of my career."

"Do you remember a patient by the name of Lucille Stanton?"

"Not clearly."

"Have you reviewed her records?"

"On November 16, 2004, when I first treated her."

"Do you remember who brought her in to see you?"

"Her niece."

"Why did she bring Ms. Stanton in?"

"She was complaining of numbness in her right hand."

"Anything else?"

"Memory loss."

"When Lucille Stanton came in to see you on November 16, how did she appear?"

"She was alert and cooperative."

"What about her speech?"

"Her speech was normal."

"Did you administer a mental exam for Ms. Stanton?"

"Yes."

"How many questions was she asked?"

"Thirty."

"Was she able to answer the questions?"

"Fourteen out of thirty."

"What does that mean?"

"It means she scored fourteen out of thirty possible."

"Okay. Was her score normal?"

"No."

"What is normal? Or, how would you characterize this fourteen-thirty score, as it relates to Lucille Stanton?"

"I would say she was moderately severely impaired cognitively." Dr. Dongohue went through the same long, boring information he had given at the deposition.

I could recite almost every major sentence he said. I knew most of it by memory—*what is moderately severe impairment?*

They can't be relied upon to care for themselves. Was Ms. Stanton given some sort of test to make this determination?

She was given a CT scan of the brain without contrast. I prided myself on retaining the scientific terms and how they related to Lucille's condition. Most of all, I knew from the deposition that Lucille couldn't have made the decision to dictate that bogus trust. The doctor was there to prove that. Or would he?

"What was the result?"

"It was indicative of small vessel disease."

"Is this common?"

"Yes."

"Was anything else shown?"

"It revealed some patchy nonconfluent, nonspecific, periventricular fluid spaces."

"Dr. Donoghue, let's go back to the Mini Mental Status Exam. Was Ms. Stanton able to understand what she read?"

"Sometimes."

"What about if the questions were read to her?"

"The same."

"How long would you say, with a medical probability, that Ms. Stanton, prior to 2004, was unable to understand what she read?" Attorney Spillinger asked.

"Probably one to two years."

"Your Honor, I have nothing else," Attorney Spillinger said.

"Thank you, Dr. Donoghue, you may step down," Judge Pinkstrom motioned.

Dr. Donoghue's words had just proved that Lucille could not have dictated the terms of the bogus trust. The text of the trust was written in complex sentences with complex meanings, and at times, Lucille couldn't understand the simplest of communications. So much precious time had been spent on the wiles of creating this injustice.

Chapter 38

The following afternoon, after Dr. Walter Donoghue had taken the witness stand, it meant that all of the witnesses had testified. Everyone who had anything to say had said it, good or bad, right or wrong, and we were all stressed and worn out.

It was whispered, though, that there was one more surprise witness. Drake and his gang looked smug. When they took the next small break in the hallway, they laughed and joked, and acted even more smug. The witness, we were told, had been instructed to go to the cafeteria and wait until the attorney called. A small rambunctious man ran up to Drake and grabbed his arm.

"She's here. She's right here in cafeteria. Right now. Right now."

"Who?"

"Juniper!"

I was shocked, but Drake jerked like someone had spotted the U.S. President walking down Main Street." Drake and his cohorts looked as if they had seen a ghost. Juniper's name hadn't been on any witness lists. Did she know something that Drake and his attorney didn't want revealed?

It was a court of law, where all the evidence should be presented. Because this case wasn't being tried by a jury, Judge Pinkstrom alone would make the ruling, based on the evidence.

Drake looked like a person taking electric shock treatments. What did Juniper know that had him in such a tizzy? Had Lucille shared information with her in those private one-on-one moments that would seal Drake's fate?

My mind pondered the myriad of things that Juniper might know. Like when she called me and told me that Drake had taken the five one hundred dollar bills from under the doily and offered her one that day we came to pick up Lucille's clothes. After that, each of her phone calls had been a road map to justice. All I had to do was to follow the crooked road. I had directed her tips to my attorney. Come to think of it, after she started calling, we didn't have to search for information at all. It just came, full and mostly accurate. Juniper's friend, Blaine Trapp, was in constant contact with Drake. So, how did he end up giving all of his information to someone who could eventually seal his fate?

As for Juniper, she must have witnessed more than she ever wanted to. But more importantly, she did own a conscience. That's how things happen when God is involved. How did she know that assisting an old lady in trouble would render enough information to vindicate that person's life, even after her death?

I was physically depleted after sitting through all the witnesses, questions, and Drake's lies. This last day was more than welcomed. I gave myself permission to take a deep breath, knowing that justice would be delivered. Or would it? I relied on the fact that life has a built-in way of bringing justice.

Now Spencer, Isabelle, Marjorie, and I were sitting in the front row. Drake reminded his attorney to make Judge Pinkstrom aware that Isabelle was a witness and should leave the room.

On this final day of the court hearing, the bailiff called the court to order. The court clerk then asked that we all rise. Judge Pinkstrom took her place on the bench.

Before Judge Pinkstrom could finish the opening ritual, Drake's attorney, Ora Mae Duffy, jumped up, almost stumbling over her words. "Your Honor, Isabelle Montague is a witness in this case. We request that she be asked to wait outside."

Before Judge Pinkstrom could comment, Attorney Spillinger spoke. "Your Honor, Isabelle Montague has already testified. I see no reason why she should not be allowed to remain in the courtroom."

Attorney Duffy blurted, "Your Honor, I'm going to call her as an impeachment witness."

We all looked at each other in shock. To impeach? For what? Attorney Duffy gave some unclear reasons to justify her request.

Judge Pinkstrom made a ruling. "Based on what I have heard, I see no reason why Ms. Montague should not be allowed to remain in the courtroom. Request denied."

"Thank you, Your Honor," Attorney Spillinger said.

Now that the fourth person who was a part of us was staying, we remained united for justice. Each of us had promised to see this to the end, and it seemed ready to happen. It was in view!

"Are you ready to proceed?" Judge Pinkstrom asked.

"Yes," both attorneys said in unison.

The six-foot, slim woman in head wrap and gold bracelets, Juniper Black, glided down front, being escorted down front by two agents. The room went quiet. Judge Pinkstrom called

Juniper to the stand without compromise or hesitation. Juniper was sworn in.

Attorney Spillinger tossed his first question to Juniper Black. "Would you state your name for the record?"

"Juniper Black." She had a smoker's voice and thin-arched eyebrows.

"Did you ever have a conversation with Elroy Bell, or did you ever hear a conversation Elroy Bell had with anyone regarding tying up Lucille Stanton's house in probate if Danielle Carrington should win the case?"

"Yes, I heard a conversation between Elroy Bell and Drake Black."

"What did you hear?"

"I was at Elroy Bell's house and had my earphone in my ear, and he thought I was taping him," Juniper answered.

"How do you know?"

"Because he asked me, 'are you taping me?'"

"And what did you say?"

"I said, 'Oh, no, this is my earphone.'"

"How did Elroy Bell plan to carry this out?"

"He planned to have Drake pay him ten thousand dollars to fix the roof, but he would say it cost fifty thousand dollars to tie up the house for years."

"Are you aware that Drake Black had filed a Restraining Order against Danielle Carrington to keep her from coming to Lucille Stanton's house?"

"Yes."

"Are you aware that you were named in the Restraining Order?"

"Yes. I found that out when I went with Drake Black to court for the hearing."

"Did Danielle Carrington ever do anything to you to cause you to apply for a Restraining Order against her?"

"No. When Drake Black asked me about putting my name on the application for the Restraining Order against Danielle, I told him that Danielle had done nothing to me and that I had no problems with her."

"Do you know anything about a living trust that Drake Black had drawn up?"

"Yes."

"Do you know who drew the trust up?"

"Yes."

"Who?"

"Elroy Bell."

"Do you remember hearing Elroy Bell tell Drake Black anything unusual about the trust?"

"Yes. After Elroy showed Drake the trust, Elroy told Drake to put Danielle Carrington's name on it."

"For what reason?"

"He said that otherwise it would look suspicious for Drake to have only his name on it. Your Honor, can I just say something?"

Juniper's question caused all of us to abruptly stop what we were doing, and I wondered what in the world she was about to say. Attorney Spillinger looked puzzled and Ora Mae Duffy's mouth was hanging open, suspended.

"Your Honor, would you please tell Mr. Black to stop 'mad dogging' me?"

That meant she was looking directly at Drake while she was testifying. From where we were sitting, we couldn't get a good read on Drake's face, but obviously Juniper could. That statement from Juniper caused me to wonder just what kind of look Drake was directing toward her.

"Mr. Black, if you are, would you please refrain from giving strange looks to Juniper Black," Judge Pinkstrom said.

I thought I had seen it all when Drake testified with his eyes closed on the first day of the trial, but after Juniper made her request to the judge, there was no telling what Drake might do. Right out of anybody's third-grade experience, Drake swiveled in his seat and turned 45 degrees so that his head faced a wall, and his back faced Juniper.

Attorney Spillinger gathered himself and resumed questioning Juniper.

"Are you aware that Drake Black moved out of Lucille Stanton's house in November of 2004?"

"Yes."

"Do you know why he left the premises?"

"Yes, he had been told to vacate the house."

"By whom?"

"Danielle Carrington had filed papers ordering him to vacate."

"So, he vacated the house in November 2004. Who told him to move back into the house one year later in December 2005?"

"Elroy Bell."

"Did you ever hear Drake Black curse or raise his voice at Lucille Stanton?"

"Yes. When she was in the kitchen trying to clean her sink that Drake had messed up, he came into the kitchen and said, "'Get your g..damn a.. outta here.'"

"What did she do after that?"

"She went and sat down in the living room, looking depressed and weeping."

"Did she say anything else?"

"Yes, she said, 'I just don't have no control over my own house no more.'"

"Did she show any other emotions at this time?"

"After that, she got a blank stare on her face and then turned her head away."

"Did you say anything to Drake when he said this to Ms. Stanton?"

"Yes. I said, 'Drake, you don't have to talk to her like that.'"

"Did Ms. Stanton express that she was afraid of Drake Black?"

"Yes."

"What did she say?"

"After one of the occasions when he hollered at her, she asked me if I would ever harm her."

"What did you tell her?"

"I told her, no. If anything, I'm gonna love you to death. I told her I didn't come to her house to harm her – just to take care of her."

"What did she do then?"

"She laid her head on my shoulder and began to cry."

"Were there any other times that Drake Black verbally abused Lucille Stanton?"

"Yes. One day, Drake and I were in Lucille's den watching TV. She came to the threshold of the door and asked if she could come in."

"What was the response?"

"Drake told her, 'No. Go back into the living room.'"

"Did you say anything to her after this?"

"I told her this was her house and she could go anywhere she wanted to."

"Were there ever any times that Lucille Stanton came to your house and stayed for extended periods of time?"

"Yes."

"Under what circumstances?"

"Drake was enrolled in school at Cyphert College, and he would bring Ms. Stanton
to my house while he attended school."

"Did he attend these classes in the day or evening?"

"Evening."

"Did this bother Lucille Stanton at all?"

"Yes. She would be very restless and would constantly complain to me and my daughters, asking us what time it was, and when Drake was coming to get her. She was so time conscious that whenever anyone told her they'd be somewhere to pick her up at a particular time, she would be on pins waiting, looking for that person to come and get her."

"Did Drake Black tell her he'd pick her up at a certain time?"

"I believe he did."

"Did he return to your house on time to pick her up?"

"No."

"Did she stop coming to your house because Drake Black completed his college courses?"

"No. After about three times, I told her that I would not put her through that any longer."

"What did you tell her?"

"I told her that I would come to her house while Drake attended school."

"What was her response?"

"She was very happy."

"Do you know whether Ms. Stanton had a set time for going to bed?"

"Yes."

"Do you know what time that was?"

"She was like a clock. She would go to bed somewhere between seven and seven-thirty each night."

"So, would you say she was displeased when she had to come to your house so Drake Black could attend school?"

"Yes."

"Did she ever make any comments about her displeasure?"

"Yes. She told me she didn't know why Drake's old self was trying to go to school anyhow."

"Did you ever have any conversations with Lucille Stanton when Drake Black was not present about her house?"

"Yes."

"And what did you say to Ms. Stanton?"

"I asked her who was going to get her house when she passed."

"And what was her response?"

"She said her niece Isabelle was getting her house."

"Did you ask her who helped her make that decision?"

"Yes."

"And what did she say?"

"She said she and her husband Nat had decided it."

"Why did she want Isabelle to have her house?"

"She said, 'Because she's crippled and don't have nothin.'"

"When junk mail would come to Lucille Stanton's house, would Ms. Stanton ask you what the mail was about?"

"Yes."

"And what would you tell her?"

"I would tell her it was people wanting to know if she wanted to sell her house."

"And what would she say?"

"She said, 'No, I don't wanna sell my house. My husband bought this house for me.'"

"Did you ever witness Drake Black giving Lucille Stanton sleeping pills?"

"Yes."

"Did she take the pills with any liquids, such as juice or water?"

"He gave her the pills with hot water."

"Why hot water?"

"He said the pills would get into her system faster."

"Do you know anything about a large sum of money found in a shoe box under Ms. Stanton's bed?"

"Yes."

"How did you come to know about the money?"

"Drake told me about the money."

"Did Drake Black ever tell you how much money was in the box?"

"Yes."

"How much money did he say was in the box?"

"Twenty-thousand dollars."

"Did he offer you some of the money?"

"Yes."

"Did you accept any of the money?"

"No."

"Did Drake Black ever mention anything to you about a safe deposit box?"

"Yes."

"What did he say?"

"He said, 'My sister says it was seventy thousand dollars in the safe deposit box, but it was only fifty thousand.'"

"Did he mention this again?"

"Yes, he repeated and said, 'It was seventy thousand dollars in the safe deposit box and twenty thousand in the shoe box under the bed.'"

"Did Drake Black ever ask you to deposit any money in your bank account for him during 2004 and 2005?"

"Yes, he asked me to put some money in my bank account for him."

"Did he tell you how much money it was he wanted you to deposit in your bank account?"

"Yes, it was ten thousand."

"What was your response?"

"I told him, no way."

"Did he ever mention this ten thousand to you again?"

"Yes, the next day he came back and told me he had gotten Eunice Black to put the money in her account."

"During 2005, did you know anything about Drake Black taking any trips?"

"Yes."

"Do you know where he went?"

"Yes. To Kentucky, Maryland, and North Carolina – wherever his ex-wife has family."

"Did he go on the trip alone?"

"No."

"Do you know who went with him?"

"Yes. His first ex-wife and his two grandsons.

"Did they drive or fly?"

"They flew."

"Lucille Stanton passed away in 2005. Did Drake Black attend her funeral?"

"Yes, but he wasn't going to."

"Who convinced him to go?"

"I did."

"That will be all. Ms. Black, you may step down."

I was speechless. In fact, everyone sat speechless. Juniper had blown the case wide open! Who could possibly know what might happen when we were asked to return for the ruling? I had thoughts of green vegetables and roasted chicken. I thought of turnip greens and cornbread. It was part and core of a good life. If money was important enough to grow deceit and lies, anger and violence, it wasn't worth anything to my life. I hadn't eaten in a long time, and now I was hungry. I could smell the freshness of young green vegetables.

Chapter 39

Because I had spoken often with Juniper prior to the trial, I knew she was full of indicting information about Drake, but how she would come across in court would be the question, or even if she would come across at all. After all, she had been Drake's second wife.

But when she began to testify, Drake's testimony was irrevocably shattered. In life, there is a truth and a lie to everything, and Juniper's testimony provided that truthfulness to the case. She had been with Lucille and Drake, even more than I. Now I was convinced that it didn't matter what the judge said, I had had my day in court. The truth had been told with clarity through the lens of a magnifying glass. The judge was the last pillar of justice. Juniper had kept the judge from being the entire pillar. Juniper's testimony had been the truth.

And, yes, today would be the moment for Judge Pinkstrom to place the seal of law to authenticate what was true, to mete out the results, punishment or payment. We never know about judges, as they set their cases inside all other cases from over the years, as examples to be cited and future cases to be measured by. Who could blame the judge if she let Drake go free? The old woman was gone; the atrocities of her treatment were not dominantly in our faces. How might the judge weigh the evidence in this case? But for me, Juniper had satisfied my first step in healing, and told me my efforts were worth the pain. One way or the other, we had won.

I wondered why Juniper had come to my soul's rescue. What did she have to gain? I also wondered if she had made her case to the judge as an innocent person concerned only with an older person's safety, playing no part in the wickedness perpetrated against Lucille. Since I had begun speaking with her after Aunt Lucille's death, I was so grateful that I had not held onto my preconceived notions about her. I was glad that I had been reasonable and forgiving enough to talk to her. To do that, I had to set aside the lies Drake had fed the family about her. In dismantling the barriers that had separated us as in-laws, I found a genuine person who possessed a soul, with compassion and conscience.

It was Tuesday, and we were all back in court—Spencer, Isabelle, Marjorie, and I.

Although the courtroom was empty, apart from the ones involved in this case, it seemed to be full. Dr. Donoghue's testimony skipped through my mind, and so did those, *I don't believe what you just said,* looks that Judge Pinkstrom gave us when Drake and Elroy testified. The court clerk and the court reporter smiled at me. I had a feeling of attachment to them, somehow. It was as if a bond of kinship, or friendship had developed between us over so much time.

I saw Judge Pinkstrom walk out of her chambers, and I hoped it would be my last sight of her. The court clerk called the courtroom to order. Judge Pinkstrom took her place on the bench. Today she looked prepared. Prepared to defend her ruling, whether it was to give Drake's trust priority over mine, or mine over his. If I should win, it meant that Lucille's house would go to her niece. If Drake should win, Lucille's house would go to Drake. Whatever winds of justice were at work would bring a ruling today.

Judge Pinkstrom read firmly and with conviction, without emotion, but with perfect enunciation. I knew that whatever her decision was there would be no changing her mind.

"In the matter of Drake Black vs. Danielle Carrington, I rule that Mr. Black held a confidence relationship with Lucille Stanton. I also rule that the testimony of Dr. Walter Donoghue was crucial in this case. The testimony of Juniper Black was pivotal in deciding this case. I find that Drake Black was not a credible witness. I find that Eunice Black was not a credible witness. I find that Elroy Bell was not a credible witness. I find that Etta Bell was not a credible witness."

There it was. The wealth of the wicked. The judge had just called all of Drake's witnesses liars. To make sure there was no confusion as to whom she meant, as she called them out, name by name. She did not name Isabelle, or Marjorie, or me. Just Drake and all of his cohorts.

She had announced, in fact, that Drake would not get a dime from the house, that Isabelle would get the house and have a place for her and her granddaughter to live, rent free, forever.

Danielle went home and wrote in her diary from her favorite chair:

> *Dear God, thank you for the experience. Thank You for Your magnificence in bringing me through it with pounding heart, weak knees and all. My fight for justice is over. Thank you.*

Epilogue

Wealth of the Wicked clarifies the means and methods by which the wicked gather wealth, and how they do not prosper in the end. It can be seen as sand running through fingers, or water that one tries to hold tight in the hand. But they seep out. They do not prosper. They're tainted. They're soiled. Someone is injured in the process of acquisition, whether it is physical, emotional, or financial injury. Wealth obtained through dishonest and deceitful means, in actuality, means the one who got wealthy was morally bankrupt.

Now that my own trial is over, I can begin the process of healing. While I was in the trial, my entire being searched only for justice, not money, not vengeance, not fame, but justice for the human condition of undeserved abuse. I sought only justice for an old woman who had been a positive influence in my life, and who had given of her youth to creating a good image of strong moral character in this world. She was paid with cruelty and pain. Some days I handle my own mental abuse about that incident better than other days, but I am healing.

I recently had occasion to be sitting in a hospital waiting room and began a conversation with another patient, who was also waiting. She told me her family's sad story. I noticed that I was hearing those horror stories of the wickedness of greed more and more frequently. The nurse walked in and began straightening the messy magazines. She told us how today there were only four magazines left out of a pile that had been there the day before.

"People are just awful. They take the magazines and think nothing of it."

The other visitor and I agreed. Then the nurse added to her story. "People come into the waiting rooms and take framed artwork from the walls." She paused. "You just can't believe it."

"How could they get the pictures out of here?" the other visitor asked.

It was a good question because the paintings that hung on the waiting room walls were pretty large, nothing a man could tuck inside his jacket, or a woman could carry in her purse. The main issue was that some individuals feel no remorse about taking pictures that belong to someone else. The nurse didn't tell us of any painting that had been returned.

But how do we, as a humane society, allow ourselves to slide into the abyss of wickedness that eventually spills over into our elderly population? The elderly deserve to be respected for their years. I say that having a trained conscience of respect and compassion is the answer to a justified life.

The perpetrators have not been taught the conscience of humanity. They feel entitled to take pictures off those walls, and to exploit their elders. They come to own that dreaded word, *entitlement.* People who are at least 70 years old have more than likely weathered life's storms, and should come to a place where they feel safe and protected. Yet, much of the harm done to them is too often perpetrated by family members.

After years of hard work, the hopes and dreams and material possessions that many have stored up for their golden years have been eaten up by greed. The unscrupulous believe the elderly should give their nest egg to them because they bring the empty signs of love. "You know I love you so much."

But for anyone who is blessed to have lived beyond the Bible's promise of three score ten years, the reality of needing someone to assist them, and not exploit them, is a huge possibility. At the time when the elderly should be comforted in knowing they will get the aid and assistance they need, they are being exploited, fearing wrath and greed, and the absence of safety and the ability to survive.

Entitlement should be considered carefully. People are entitled to a paycheck only after working an honest day's work. Entitlement is not a gift; it's a right that should come from effort. A gift is not worked for. It's something that is given voluntarily, without a charge. It is something that someone wants you to have. You are not entitled to a gift. Otherwise, it changes the very meaning of what a gift is. Salvation is freely given to all who will receive it. It's a gift from God. There's nothing we can do to earn it.

We seem to have become a society of piranhas that prey on our elderly. Is it due to mindset or conscience? Yes, it comes from people who have allowed life to pass them by when they should have been storing up. They find themselves without the finances to take care of themselves, and they turn to the aged to compensate for their bad choices. I say, the aged have no responsibility for them at all. But the elderly are seeking love and companionship, and they are vulnerable. It is in their changed nature to accept nice red apples that may, in fact, contain worms.

Most seniors have absolutely no energy to defend themselves. But because their energy is not there, should they be exploited in the last days of their lives on earth? I think not.

I wrote this book because of a real-life situation in my own family that shocked me and changed my life's view forever. I wrote a fictional version of my situation to put a face on the 1.2 million senior citizens who face physical, emotional, and financial abuse every year. My story is written to illuminate the problem and offer methods of healing such injustice. It calls on decent human beings to recognize such injustice and fight against it.

Pride, arrogance, greed, and fraud are the character traits by which we can identify bankrupt perpetrators who are willing, even anxious to abuse the elderly. Someone might ask, how can one be bankrupt, and yet have money? That's because any wealth attained by harming another person is not true wealth. It lasts for a moment and slips away, and it is seen no more.

In Wealth of the Wicked, the characters created to tell my story are not real. Their names have been changed to protect the innocent. My characters were created to best dramatize my family's story.

Drake Black played Lucille Stanton like a Stradivarius violin. He was smooth as a bottle of aged wine. Lucille Stanton didn't have a clue about the harm that was being perpetrated against her. It shouldn't be assumed that she could have prevented that unimaginable situation. She had lost the ability to defend herself. She was too innocent, forgetful, and forgiving, and too old.

Such cruel life occurrences are never without residual debris. It is one of the tragedies resulting from many storms. They leave the elderly and those who care for them with many moments of sadness. They leave families like mine so broken they seem impossible to mend. In the case of families like mine, there is someone you thought you knew, a person you've lived with and played with, and they become nothing more than a cruel stranger driven by greed.

The story on which I based my book deeply wounded me. Four years later, the emotional scars still resurface, fewer now than before. There are still triggers that I'm fighting to overcome. My husband and my children have not gone unscathed either. But I have made a conscious decision not to be battered and bruised by it any more. That incident cannot take any more of my life, nor any more of my family's lives.

In many ways, I wrote this book to honor my dad, who passed away a while ago. I do wonder whether children ever think about how their parents would feel about how they turned out. I'm firmly convinced that just because the classroom in the home is open for instruction, it does not mean that everyone attending comes for the same reasons. Some do come to learn. Others come because they are commanded. They sit and pretend they're taking in the lessons, but they learn early to lie. Later they perfect the lies. Then the lies become who they are.

I wrote this book in a dramatic way for the reader to experience the horror of abuse, to take up the conscience to protect loved ones from abuse. As a society, we must find ways to protect our loved ones, especially after they retire and just want to live in peace. If airtight plans are not in place, the senior's desire to enjoy a peaceful existence might well be interrupted by individuals who feel *entitled* to what the senior has.

I encourage my readers to watch for the warning signs of elder abuse. Listed, you will find local, state, and federal resources to help you make logical decisions at the first sign of trouble. Don't be afraid, or ashamed to talk to government and nonprofit agencies that I have used and/or researched. If you need me to speaker on this subject to your organization, I am available, and can be reached at:

jlauderdale@newimagewriters.com

janicelauderdale@yahoo.com.

www.writethewrong1.com

References

10 WARNING SIGNS OF DANGER FOR THE ELDERLY

1. Unusual forgetfulness—the first sign of forgetfulness have the elderly person you love to list their assets and liabilities
2. Personal neglect—see if you can interest the elderly person to go to the local senior citizen center to meet other people and take an interest in a hobby. Assure them that they need to look nice to meet people—bathed, hair combed, clean and fitted clothes
3. Forgetting where they are—give them pegs to help them remember where they are
4. Always living in the past—always talk about familiar family members and events in the present, leading up from the past
5. Not recognizing family members—let them see people often, and recall the past with them in the picture
6. Doctor reports severe Dementia/Alzheimer's—it is time to act, even before this stage
7. Telling you things you know are not true—this is a sign that the mind is in decline and the one caring for the person, even on a part-time basis, should make arrangements for full-time care
8. Getting irritable for no reason--
9. Suspicious of those who love them
10. Being unreasonable in their demands

15 WARNING SIGNS OF CHOOSING THE CARETAKER

1. You cannot trace his/her past
2. Scant references without past work record
3. Unstable past

4. No means of support
5. Seems too nice to be true
6. Harsh manners immediately after take over
7. Rushed to move in
8. Immediately seeks financial information
9. Notice immediate decline of the elderly
10. Elderly person seems afraid to talk and uncomfortable around the caretaker
11. No planned meal or bedtime routine
12. No planned outings
13. Leaves alone for long periods of time
14. Drags the elderly person around for his or her convenience
15. Cannot show any record of medication schedule

When you have more than three of those characteristics, it's time to look farther.

18 STEPS FOR PROTECTING THE ELDERLY

1. List all assets and liabilities
2. List insurances
3. List all legal, medical, business, monies due, amount
4. List all monthly payments
5. List who will be in charge of business
6. List all wishes of who will take care of him or her, where he/she will live
7. List the wishes of property disposal—children/who/how much to each, charities, educational institutions
8. What to do with her remains—burial—where, cremation or ground, crypt, donate to science
9. Count and list cash in safe deposit box—remove and put in an interest-bearing account

10. Arrange a legal Living Trust with an attorney based on the list above
11. Seek legal advice on locating any Intellectual Property, such as songs, plays, books, set up who will be responsible for taking care of it
12. Decide who will be the caretaker—person, family, assisted living, senior community
13. Get a Power of Attorney
14. Assisted living—visit the patients and talk with them
15. Visit the facility often
16. Take your senior to visit a senior community more than once
17. Allow the well senior to return on his or her own
18. Finding a reliable care taker

11 WARNING STEPS IN SELECTING THE CARETAKER

1) Put everything in writing
2) Run a credit check
3) Have your attorney investigate his/her background
4) Get 3-5 business and personal references
5) Create a list of written questions
6) Look for a past of violence
7) Look for a past of neglect
8) Look for a pattern of abuse
9) Look for lies or inconsistencies in their answers
10) Check out every reference
11) Family members do not escape the routine

Elderly Abuse Statistics

While statistics indicate a very high incident of elder abuse, it is almost unheard of it that it is talked about it in families, or punished by the law. It is Janice Lauderdale's intent to show the ugly face of elder abuse and make the responsible government agencies and families aware of the grave problem. She intends to show some simple things that can help avoid such incidents. She wishes to open up a heightened awareness of such criminal offenses. It is her intention to hold hearings before congress to ask their favor of more support to this segment of society, who are not really the numbers listed below, but our grandmothers, grandfathers and close and dear relatives.

www.karisable.com/elder
"Every year an estimated 1.2 million older Americans are victims of physical, psychological, or other forms of abuse and neglect. For every case of elder abuse and neglect reported to authorities, experts estimate that there may be as many as 5 cases not reported. Research suggests elders who have been abused tend to die earlier than those who are not abused, even in the absence of chronic conditions or life threatening disease."

"Americans over the age of 50 years represent 30% of our population, 12% of our murder victims and 7% of other serious and violent crime victims."

"90% of elder abuse and neglect incidents are by known perpetrators, usually family members, 2/3rds are adult children or spouses, 42% of murder victims over 60 were killed by their own offspring. Spouses were the perpetrators in 24% of family murders of persons over 60."

"The eldest of our seniors, 80 years and older are abused and neglected at 2-3 times the proportion of all other senior citizens."

www.aoa.gov/eldfam

The largest category of perpetrators (47.3%) of the substantiated incidents of elder abuse was the adult children of the victims. Spouses represented the second largest group of perpetrators comprising 19.3%. In addition, other relatives were the third most frequent category of perpetrators (8.8%), with grandchildren following closely (8.6%).

Relationship of perpetrators to victims of domestic abuse:

Child	47%
Sibling	6%
Grandchild	9%
Spouse	19%
Other relative	9%
Parent	0%
Friend/Neighbor	6%
In-home Service Provider	3%
Out-of-home Service Provider	1%

www.safestate.org

Statistics uncover a frightening picture of elder and dependent adult abuse in California. In the last few years, according to the California Department of Social Services, the statewide number of abuse reports has grown by 23 percent, from 75,843 in 2000-01 to 93,517 in 2005-06. Unfortunately, more than two-thirds of abusers are family members.

Currently, it is estimated that only one in five cases is reported within our state. Nationally, one of every 20 elderly people will be abused in their lifetime. With more than 3.7 million Californians 65 or elder, and an expected population growth to 6.3 million by 2018, the incidents of elder and dependent adult abuse are likely to grow…if we don't take action.

Anyone who suspects that a senior is being victimized should call local law enforcement or the statewide toll-free elder abuse reporting hotline at 1-888-436-3600.

www.avhotline.org

According to a 2004 study done by The National Committee for the Prevention of Elder Abuse and The National Adult Protective Services Association…

Self neglect accounts for about 38% of elder abuse, 20% is due to caregiver neglect, 15% is due to financial exploitation.

About 33% of abusers were the children of the victim. About 22% were other family members of the victim.

www.neve.org

- There are presently about 39 million individuals over the age of 65; the U.S. Census Bureau projects that more than 62 million Americans will be 65 or older in 2025.

- Older women (67%) are far more likely than men (32%) to suffer from abuse and slightly more than half of the alleged perpetrators of elder abuse were female (53%). (National Center on Elder Abuse Study, 2004).

- Twenty percent of elder abuse involved caregiver neglect; 15% centered on emotional, psychological, or verbal abuse; 15% involved financial exploitation; 11% was physical abuse, and 1% was sexual abuse (Teaster, National Center on Elder Abuse, 2006).

- In 2004, Adult Protective Services received a total of 565,747 reports of elder abuse for persons of all ages from 50 states, plus Guam and the District of Columbia, and investigated 461,135 reports. Of that number, APS substantiated 191,908 reports of elder abuse for victims of all ages, representing a 16% increase from the 2000 survey. (National Center on Elder Abuse Study, 2004).

- Because older victims usually have fewer support systems and reserves – physical, psychological, and economic– the impact of abuse and neglect is magnified, and a single incident of mistreatment is more likely to trigger a downward spiral leading to loss of independence, a serious complicating illness, and even death. (Burgess and Hanrahan, 2006).

- Of alleged perpetrators of elder abuse, 33% were adult children, 22% were other family members; 1% were strangers, and 11% were spouses/intimate partners (Teaster, National Center on Elder Abuse, 2006).

Living Trust

A living trust is an absolute must for an elderly or incapacitated family member. Although it is more expense than a will, the potential heartache and pain brought on by not having one is heartache unlike you've ever experienced. A will can definitely be contested. A living trust is more full proof against someone contesting the contents.

In my particular case, I dare say if a living trust was not already in place, upon my aunt's death, and by my brother obtaining a bogus trust, in court he would have gotten the last thing he so desperately wanted – the house. The point is, according to my understanding of the law, if there are two competing Trusts the last trust drawn up trumps the first one. But, in my particular situation, after spending thousands of dollars, the court declared after the testimony of his countless less than truthful witnesses, the trust he had drawn up was bogus and thus it was invalidated by the court.

What were some of the elements contained in that trust making it invalid or certainly questioning the circumstances under which it was drawn up?

- At the time the second trust was drafted, the Trustor was suffering from Alzheimer's of the dementia type and not capable of making sound decisions.

- Not in a mental place to name beneficiaries.

- Because there was an existent Trust obtained in the year 2000, the court ruled that the bogus trust was signed under duress.

- This is a legal document and must, by law, be notarized.

- "Do you understand everything I'm telling you" was the question asked of the elderly person. What would she say, except "Yea?"

- If they are suffering from the effects of Alzheimer's and any related illness, how are they going to give consent to something so important? They hardly know who they are.

- After she was coaxed to the neighbor's house where the notary was present and after signing the phony documents she says, "Now they can't take my house." The judge surmised that she wouldn't have, in her condition, said that.

- The notary should never have completed and signed-off on the document. The elderly person was incapable of understanding and answering the questions she was being asked.

- The original trust had been drafted some four years before naming some 12+ people as beneficiaries. She was mentally healthy.

- Second trust was drafted naming only the nephew as beneficiary. Clearly, the judge saw that greed had taken over.

- When the second trust which was bogus was drafted she was in a state of mental decline. Not capable of making sound decisions.
- Her choices should not have been questioned.
- It's criminal to obtain another Trust simply because you don't agree with the original one. Further, it was morally wrong and criminal to take someone else's money without their conscious consent.

Breinigsville, PA USA
05 November 2010
248753BV00001B/1/P